Longman Study Texts

D0801241

Animal Farm

Longman Study Texts

General editor: Richard Adams

Titles in the series:

George Orwell

Animal Farm

edited by
Robert Wilson

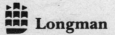 **Longman**

LONGMAN GROUP UK LIMITED
Longman House
Burnt Mill, Harlow, Essex, CM20 2JE, England
and Associated Companies throughout the world.

ISBN 0-582-33087-4

First published by Martin Secker and Warburg 1945
This edition first published in the Longman Study Texts 1983
by permission of Martin Secker and Warburg

Ninth impression 1993
This impression 1993

Set in 10/12 pt. Linotron 202 Baskerville

Reprinted under licence from Longman Group Ltd.
Not for sale outside Zimbabwe

This edition is in memory of John Hutchings

Produced by Longman Group (FE) Ltd
Printed by National Printing and Packaging, Harare, Zimbabwe

Contents

Introduction

George Orwell's life

More than in most cases, the writing career of George Orwell is inseparable from his life experience. He commented very directly on the society and times in which he lived and his strong feelings about social injustice and oppression were the main motivating force behind all his writings, whether essays, pieces of journalism, novels or semi-autobiographical documentaries. He was far from being just an intellectual producing his books during a life of retirement and quiet. On the contrary, Orwell was a policeman in Burma; he was a tramp in England and a dishwasher in a Parisian restaurant; he lived with poor working-class people and experienced their lives at first hand; he fought in the Spanish Civil War; he kept a village shop and for a short time lived a virtually self-sufficient life on a remote island in the Hebrides; and all this was in addition to writing and broadcasting and developing a wide circle of literary and politically-minded friends in London. We can catch glimpses of the life of this man of action and experience by imagining ourselves viewing some characteristic moments through a series of snapshots.

Our first snapshot is of the nine-year-old Eric Blair (for that is how we must call him until he assumes his pen name of George Orwell on the publication of his first novel) dressed in the uniform of an English preparatory school, St. Cyprian's, which was near Eastbourne, and the year is 1912. His presence in such a school suggests his middle-class background. In fact, he had been born in 1903 in Burma where his father was an official in the Indian Civil Service but his mother had brought him and his sister to England in 1904, for it was the custom for the children of Anglo-Indians (the British in India) to be brought up and educated in England. Eric is not looking particularly happy in our imaginary snapshot, and later in life

George Orwell was able to state clearly the reasons for his unhappiness at St. Cyprian's. One reason was that his family was
less wealthy than the families of the other boys; he came from
what he was to call the 'lower-upper-middle-class' who strug-
gled to maintain the appearance of gentility without having the
resources to do it properly. The result is the 'shabby-genteel'
style and the sort of unhappiness felt by Gordon Cornstock in
Orwell's novel *Keep the Aspidistra Flying*:

> Even at the third-rate schools to which Gordon was sent
> nearly all the boys were richer than himself. They soon
> found out his poverty, of course, and gave him hell because
> of it. Probably the greatest cruelty one can inflict on a child
> is to send him to a school among children richer than him-
> self. A child conscious of poverty will suffer snobbish agonies
> such as a grown-up person can scarcely imagine.

Orwell's later hatred of the English class system can perhaps
be traced back to these early experiences.

The other reason for Eric Blair's unhappiness at St. Cyprian's is the way in which the school is run. In his autobio-
graphical essay 'Such, Such were the Joys', Orwell describes the
rigid and hated rules, the unfair punishments and beatings of a
school dominated by the headmaster's wife whose inconsistent
and rapidly changing moods meant that the happiness or hell
of the boys depended entirely on her whim. Orwell describes 'a
sense of desperate loneliness and helplessness, of being locked
up not only in a hostile world but in a world of good and evil
where the rules were such that it was actually not possible for
me to keep them...it was not possible for me to be good'.
Here is a model of the totalitarian society that Orwell was later
to criticise in *Animal Farm* and *Nineteen Eighty-Four*, a state
which is dominated by a single tyrant who manipulates all the
resources of the country and plays on the guilt and fear of
ordinary people so as to satisfy his sense of power. The un-

happiness on the face of the young Eric Blair in our first snapshot is the origin of his political beliefs and the source of his life-long concern to side with the underdog.

Let us move on ten years, to 22 October 1922; the place is Birkenhead and Blair is leaning on the rail of the *S. S. Hertfordshire*, a passenger steamer about to depart for Rangoon, in Burma, where he will join the Imperial Indian Police. He is nineteen, a tall young man with a podgy face and a grin that reveals uncertainty. He is thoughtful, thin and rather gangling and his clothes hang on him in an untidy way. He has just spent six months hard labour at a crammers preparing for the India Office's examinations, having survived an undistinguished career at Eton, to which he had won a scholarship in 1917. Eton has, however, given him freedom to make friends and to explore popular liberal and socialist ideas, for these are the years of reaction against the patriotic and authoritarian attitudes that had led up to the First World War. Widely read but unformed in his opinions, Blair is an enigma at this moment in his career. We doubt that he is feeling a sense of adventure, excitement and commitment as he takes up 'the White Man's burden':

To wait in heavy harness,
On fluttered folk and wild –
Your new-caught, sullen peoples,
Half-devil and half-child.

These words of Kipling express the mood of patriotic and condescending dedication with which young men went East to serve the Empire. It is more likely that Blair, having avoided work at Eton and any attempt to enter Oxford University, is dutifully following his father's career and is probably aware that he will not like the course he has to pursue. Certainly there was to be at least one incident in this voyage out of which must have begun that process of questioning and criticism of the British in India which was to lead him to resign from the service five years later. In 1940, in an article he wrote for the magazine *Time and Tide*, Orwell recalled

> the first sight I saw when I set foot on the soil of Asia – or rather, just before setting foot there. The liner I was travelling in was docking at Colombo, and the usual swarm of coolies had come aboard to deal with the luggage. Some policemen, including a white sergeant, were superintending them. One of the coolies had got hold of a long tin uniform-case and was carrying it so clumsily as to endanger people's heads. Someone cursed at him for his carelessness. The police sergeant looked round, saw what the man was doing, and caught him a terrific kick on the bottom that sent him staggering across the deck. Several passengers, including women, murmured their approval.

That article carries the message of a convinced socialist who is clear in his condemnation of oppression in all its forms, but the Eric Blair of our second snapshot is not, in 1922, at all certain of his stand. As a policeman in Burma he was to suffer the frustration of carrying out an authoritarian role that he disapproved of and like Flory, the hero of his novel *Burmese Days*, he must have sometimes felt hatred for his own hypocrisy:

> Year after year you sit in Kipling-haunted little Clubs, whisky to right of you, *Pink'un* to left of you, listening and eagerly agreeing while Colonel Bodger develops his theory that these bloody Nationalists should be boiled in oil. You hear your oriental friends called 'greasy little babus', and you admit, dutifully, that they *are* greasy little babus. You see louts fresh from school kicking greyhaired servants. The time comes when you burn with hatred of your own countrymen, when you long for a native rising to drown their Empire in blood.

Our third imaginary snapshot was taken in October 1929,

almost exactly seven years after the second. Eric Blair is to be seen bending over a sink, washing endless piles of dishes. This is the kitchen of a Parisian restaurant, a dirty, hot, over-crowded place, full of panic, confusion, angry demands and sheer physical exhaustion. It is at least a thirteen-hour work-day and Blair has been reduced to this slavery because, not finding work in Paris, he has pawned his good clothes and, having pawned them, he can only apply for the most menial of jobs. He has chosen to put himself into this condition of servile poverty because of a desire and a personal need to experience degradation and hardship. Later, in *The Road to Wigan Pier*, he explained his motives:

> I felt that I had got to escape not merely from imperialism but from every form of man's dominion over man. I wanted to submerge myself, to get right down among the oppressed; to be one of them and on their side against the tyrants. And, chiefly because I had had to think everything out in solitude, I had carried my hatred of oppression to extraordinary lengths.

That was Blair's state of mind when he returned to England from Burma but, first, having decided that he wanted to be a writer, he had simply found cheap lodgings and started writing. It was not very successful because he had nothing very pressing to write about and so it is likely that the two years or so that he spent tramping and living with the destitute, at first in London and then in Paris, were as much a quest for experience as a purging of guilty feelings at having had a middle-class background. The venture had begun in 1927 when he had gone to a poor second-hand shop and bought a set of ragged old clothes. An incident in *The Road to Wigan Pier* conveys the excitement of his new situation:

> My new clothes had put me instantly into a new world. Everyone's demeanour seemed to have changed abruptly. I

helped a hawker pick up a barrow that he had upset. 'Thanks, mate,' he said with a grin. No one had called me mate before in my life – it was the clothes that had done it.

The anecdote gives us a taste of the exhilaration that Blair must have felt at this newly discovered freedom and it is easy to understand how, once he had begun to go native as a brief experiment, it would lead on to the more serious and lengthy period of destitution in Paris.

Let us move on another seven years, to February 1936, when our fourth glimpse into the life of this remarkable man is through the eyes of Joe Kennan, an active Labour Party worker, living in Wigan and working in the coal mines. In a B.B.C. Television 'Omnibus' programme of 1970, he describes meeting Eric Blair:

> There was a knock at the door on Saturday afternoon. We were just having tea. And I opened the door and there was this tall fella with a pair of flannel bags on, a fawn jacket and a mac. And he told me he had two letters, one from Middleton Murry, who was a pacifist author ... (He) wanted me to find him a type of lodgings of a lower class, practically of a slum character.... I introduced him to some of the lads connected with the Unemployed Workers' Movement ... they did find him these lodgings.

What is Blair doing in Wigan and what has happened to him over the last seven years, since we saw him slaving away as a *plongeur* in Paris? To begin with, he has had a variety of jobs: as a private tutor, a preparatory school master, a hop-picker in Kent, an assistant in a left-wing bookshop in Hampstead and, above all, as a writer. His writing career has begun with reviewing work for the magazine *The Adelphi* and his first book, *Down and Out in Paris and London*, has been published in 1933. It is based on the tramping experiences about which we have heard, and since there is obviously a conflict between his experiences and attitudes and those of his family, he has assumed the pseudonym George Orwell, to avoid embarrassment to his relatives. Two more semi-autobiographical novels have followed: *Burmese Days* (published in 1934) and *A Clergyman's Daughter* (1935) and now, in February 1936, he has just finished some last-minute changes to the manuscript of *Keep the Aspidistra Flying*, another novel. He is an established author who is becoming well known in literary circles. He has met a number of influential writers and he has begun to write regularly for *The New English Weekly*. Moreover, he has met an intelligent and attractive young woman called Eileen O'Shaughnessy whom he intends to marry. But it is a measure of his success as a writer that he has come to Wigan, commissioned by the publisher Victor Gollancz, on an advance of £500, to write a book about the conditions of the unemployed in the industrial north of England.

The Road to Wigan Pier was to be the outcome of the couple of months that Orwell spent in the north. The first part of the book describes the squalor and demoralisation of the working class life that he saw there. His anger reaches us through sights such as this, seen from the train leaving Wigan:

As we moved slowly through the outskirts of the town we passed row after row of little grey slum houses running at right angles to the embankment. At the back of one of the houses a young woman was kneeling on the stones, poking a stick up the leaden waste-pipe which ran from the sink inside and which I suppose was blocked. I had time to see everything about her – her sacking apron, her clumsy clogs, her arms reddened by the cold. She looked up as the train passed, and I was almost near enough to catch her eye. She had a round pale face, the usual exhausted face of the slum girl who is twenty-five and looks forty, thanks to miscarriages and drudgery; and it wore, for the second in which I saw it, the most desolate, hopeless expression I have ever seen .... She knew well enough what was happening to her –

understood as well as I did how dreadful a destiny it was to be kneeling there in the bitter cold, on the slimy stones of a slum backyard; poking a stick up a foul drain-pipe.

It was sights such as this that prompted Orwell to clarify his own political views and committed him to left-wing socialism but not, in the end, to communism. His anger at the suffering of ordinary people became the political concern for the oppressed that was to be so movingly presented in *Animal Farm*.

If we pass on now to our fifth snapshot of George Orwell, we see him in a very different situation. It is exactly a year after his visit to Wigan and he is in the trenches of the front line in Spain, participating in the Spanish Civil War, fighting alongside the Republicans against Franco. He is a company commander in the P.O.U.M. (Partido Obrero de Unificación Marxista), a marxist party which has its own small and ill-equipped militia but is not dominated by Russian Communists. In a B.B.C. broadcast of 2 November 1960, Bob Edwards gives us a vivid glimpse of Orwell's appearance:

All six foot three of him was striding towards me and his clothing was grotesque to say the least. He wore riding breeches, khaki puttees and huge boots. I've never seen boots that were so large, clogged in mud. He had a yellow pigskin jerkin, a coffee-coloured balaclava hat and he wore the longest scarf I've ever seen; a khaki scarf wrapped round and round his neck right up to his ears. On his shoulder he carried an old-fashioned German rifle; I think it must have been fifty years old; and hanging to his belt were two hand grenades. Running beside him, trying to keep pace, were two youths of the Militia, similarly equipped; but what amused me most was that behind Orwell was a shaggy mongrel dog with the word POUM painted on its side.

His courage and daring in the fighting in Spain have been commented on by many of his contemporaries. What the

P.O.U.M. lacked in uniforms, equipment, weapons or ammunition, it made up for in courage and idealism and Orwell relished the part he played in a fraternity of all nationalities brought together in the effort to oppose tyranny, the totalitarian state.

Orwell was soon to be wounded in the throat and eventually taken back to Barcelona where he and his wife (for he had married Eileen on 9 June 1936 and she had come out to Spain in the following February) were involved in fighti.g which suddenly broke out between different groups of revolutionary militias. In spite of putting their own lives in great danger in an effort to get one of their comrades released from prison, the Orwells managed to escape from Spain in late June 1937.

Homage to Catalonia is Orwell's account of his experiences in the Spanish Civil War. It is a vivid piece of reporting and it also denounces the cynical Russian power politics which stirred up the fighting in Barcelona and betrayed a popular revolution that might otherwise have given the working classes true freedom and status. Propaganda and false reporting, deception of the people and the theme of the revolution betrayed were later to find their most convincing expression in *Animal Farm* and *Nineteen Eighty-Four*. The Spanish war had a profound effect on Orwell and his beliefs. As he, himself, said,

The Spanish war and other events in 1936–37 turned the scale and thereafter I knew where I stood. Every line of serious work that I have written since 1936 has been written, directly or indirectly, against totalitarianism and for democratic Socialism, as I understand it.

('Why I Write')

In other words, Orwell had come to see the evil of any totalitarian state. He saw that Russian Communism dominated by Stalin was as evil and oppressive as fascism in Germany or Spain, dominated by Hitler or Franco. These are the ideas behind *Animal Farm*; but before we come to the years in which that novel was written, there is one other snapshot to be taken.

It is the surprising picture of a village shopkeeper in Hertfordshire, enjoying his place in the local community and also keeping a vegetable garden, hens and a goat. Orwell had acquired the village shop in Wallington, Hertfordshire, immediately after his time in Wigan and just before his marriage to Eileen. After their return from Spain, he was for some time seriously ill from tuberculosis, the disease which was eventually to kill him, but in the spring of 1939 they were relieved to return at last to Wallington. Orwell always sought the simple, practical life and avoided the race to acquire money, possessions and power. This snapshot of him in Wallington stands for a relatively brief period of his life but it is an important one because it indicates how much he wished to live the ideals about which he wrote. Poverty for him meant freedom, freedom to be himself and not to be identified with a class and, of course, freedom to write. *Coming Up for Air*, published in 1939, was his next novel, an attempt to arouse people to assume a responsible attitude towards the coming war and to the acquisitive society that he saw destroying the quality of life.

With the onset of the war against Nazi Germany in 1939, we approach our seventh relevant snapshot glimpse of Orwell. Unable to join up because of his tuberculosis and increasing ill-health, he was forced to confine his own war effort to joining the Home Guard and taking a job with the B.B.C. where he worked in the Indian Service. It is characteristic that he and his wife should have moved into London for the more useful work that they could do there. They were in central London all through the tense summer of the Battle of Britain when it looked as though England would be invaded by Hitler's forces, and then through the long winter suffering of the bombing of London. Orwell continued to write and broadcast regularly and he greatly increased his range of friends and acquaintances, particularly amongst literary men. In his autobiography, *Almost A Gentleman*, Mark Benney gives us our snapshot glimpse of what life was like in those frightening years. He describes an evening spent with the Orwells:

> We had just taken our places at the dining table under the big 'picture' window when a bomb fell some fifty yards away and we were lifted out of our seats by the blast. When we picked ourselves up, the room was covered with the fine splinters from the shattered window, and the only light came from the incendiary bombs burning in the street outside, but none of us was hurt. Eileen said, incredulously, 'No, no – not *again*!' I said, looking with relief at the bottle still in my hand, 'At least the wine's safe!' Eric said glumly, 'If we'd been in one of those working-class hovels round the corner we'd be as dead as mutton now!'

Typically, Orwell related every experience firmly back to his overriding concern for the poor: his political awareness was the product of too much felt experience to be shifted by the mere explosion of a bomb.

Animal Farm was written between November 1943 and February 1944 when the danger of defeat was waning, Germany was exhausting herself in Russia and being beaten back in Europe and Orwell was feeling the glow of success and the pleasure of useful employment. All this contributed to the tone of the new novel which, as we shall see, is a skilful blend of sharp criticism on the one hand, and lightness, charm and pathos on the other. The criticism is directed towards Soviet Russia and its totalitarian regime under Stalin. It was not, therefore, surprising that publishers were slow to accept *Animal Farm*, for at this stage in the war Russia was an ally of Britain and the U.S.A. It was finally published in August 1945 and was immediately successful.

The closing years of the war were demanding times in other ways for Orwell. He and Eileen adopted a baby son and then, early in 1945, Orwell went to France to report on the final stages of the war for *The Observer*. Always ready for the life of action, he was delighted to have this opportunity to participate in the war from which he had been excluded by his ill-health but the venture was to be sadly cut short for, on 29th March, Eileen died during an operation for cancer. Famous and financially secure at last, it is ironic that Orwell in the final years of his life should have been deprived of the companionship and love of his wife and of good health. His tuberculosis became much worse. Nor was his health helped by the remoteness of the place he now chose to make his home – the island of Jura in the Hebrides off the west coast of Scotland – and the inevitable lack of medical attention on the island. However, he relished the simple, practical life that he was able to enjoy but briefly on Jura and the quiet and remoteness from the journalistic bustle of London. It gave him the peace in which he could write his final novel, *Nineteen Eighty-Four*.

In *Nineteen Eighty-Four*, the gentle humour of *Animal Farm* has turned into a frighteningly serious warning of the physical horrors and spiritual torture of living under a regime that combines the techniques of Communism with those of Nazism for the purpose of keeping a small group of power-hungry party members in absolute power. Orwell presents the world as divided into power blocks that are maintained in a state of endless fighting and endless shortages. This grim and pessimistic warning of what might happen if men give up their freedom for the apparent economic security of living in a totalitarian state was completed when Orwell's health was finally breaking. He forced himself to type the final version of the book in spite of terrible pain and weakness and the effort brought on the final phase of his illness. He came back to England and went into a sanatorium in the Cotswolds. Finally, he was moved to University College Hospital, London.

It is here, in a small private room, that we take our last snapshot of George Orwell. It is October 13th 1949 at about noon. Orwell, gaunt and ill, is dressed surprisingly in a crimson corduroy smoking jacket. It makes him look unusually grand, like a retired army officer. Around him is a group of his closest friends including the writers Malcolm Muggeridge and Anthony Powell, the newspaper proprietor David Astor and Sonia Brownell, who is a very attractive woman of thirty-one. They are all very joyful and Orwell is exuberant for today, in this hospital room, by 'special licence' he has married Sonia. He confidently expects to go to a sanatorium in Switzerland in a few months' time and to recover from his tuberculosis sufficiently to be able to write for a few hours every day.

It was not to be. He never left University College Hospital, for on the night of 21 January 1950 his lung haemorrhaged. He died at once.

The ideas behind Animal Farm

In 1947 Orwell wrote a preface for a Ukrainian edition of *Animal Farm*; in this he explained why he wrote the book and how the idea of it came to him:

On my return from Spain I thought of exposing the Soviet myth in a story that could be easily understood by almost anyone and which could be easily translated into other languages. However, the actual details of the story did not come to me for some time until one day (I was then living in a small village) I saw a little boy, perhaps ten years old, driving a huge cart-horse along a narrow path, whipping it whenever it tried to turn. It struck me that if only such animals became aware of their strength we should have no power over them, and that men exploit animals in much the same way as the rich exploit the proletariat.

He makes it clear that *Animal Farm* is essentially a serious book about politics, one which is directly concerned to expose the wholly false view of the Russian Revolution which was held by western communists and communist sympathisers. In order to understand the book we must therefore clarify not only what were Orwell's own political views but also the differences between socialism and communism.

Socialism refers, in general, to any system of organising a society in which goods and property are owned by the society as a whole rather than by individuals. These are not new ideas – Plato in the fourth century B.C. described such a system in his *Republic* and the early Christians also practised corporate ownership – but in its modern forms socialism does not insist on the abolition of private property although it does advocate that the government should own the *means* of production, that is, the industries that transform raw materials into the things we need. A socialist also believes that the way to achieve public ownership is through legal and constitutionally acceptable methods. So, for example, the British Labour Party has a policy of purchasing industries from private firms and 'nationalising' them, that is, making their running the responsibility of the government. By this means, a socialist believes that wealth will be more evenly distributed through society. On the other hand, Orwell, along with many other socialists, was firmly of the belief that although socialism was the only hope there was of improving the quality of life for all people, it could not and should not claim to be able to make things perfect. We call the idea of a perfect society a utopia; socialism, according to Orwell, should offer realistic hopes of improvement, not utopian idealism.

Some of the differences between socialism and communism will have already become evident to you. Firstly, whereas in a socialist society individuals may retain private property, communism seeks to abolish all private possessions. Secondly, communism advocates the taking of ownership and control of industry and government by means of violent revolution, but socialism attempts to achieve public ownership and social change by legal means and without a revolution. Thirdly, socialism does not claim to be able to make things perfect but communism is idealistic. Its ideas are mainly the inspiration of

Karl Marx, a German economist, and he was an idealist, dreaming of a utopian paradise in which all men should be free and equal.

So what is wrong with idealism? Why should Orwell want to condemn these dreams of a utopia? The answer is that this very idealism allowed for the emergence of a frightening and repressive dictatorship in Russia, every bit as bad as the dictatorships established by Hitler and Mussolini in fascist countries. We need to consider Marx's ideas in a little more detail to see how this could happen.

Marx believed that capitalists, the people who own industries, are no longer necessary and that their existence actually causes the suffering of the working people who make up the largest number of people in society. His solution was for the workmen to take over the means of production through violent revolution. Private property must not be permitted after the revolution for that would allow clever men eventually to claim the means of production, to take control of industry and so become new capitalists. To make sure that this did not happen, Marx advocated that after the revolution, a country should be governed by what he called a 'dictatorship of the common man'. In practice this meant the rule of those who were members of the Communist Party but after a period this dictatorship would, he believed, gradually disappear, leaving all men free and equal. The problem was that Marx never explained how this 'dictatorship of the common man' would wither away. Instead it turned into tyranny.

During the years between the two world wars, years of great hardship and economic difficulty, many intellectuals and writers in England were socialists searching for a better way of organising the world than that which was producing so much poverty and deprivation around them. Since communism is, from one point of view, only an extreme form of socialism, Western socialists faced a problem in knowing how to react to Soviet Russia which was at that time the only government in the world based on completely socialist principles. They felt they should give it some support even if they disagreed with part of its theory and way of operating.

Orwell gradually came to realise, largely through his experiences in the Spanish Civil War, that such support of Soviet Russia would be entirely misplaced. He saw that the communist state had been established on the basis of an impossible dream which had simply misled the people and that a group of clever leaders were controlling, manipulating and exploiting the common people simply to keep themselves in power and ease. He saw too that out of that group of leaders had emerged a single dictator – Stalin – who had become a tyrant and was organising the whole state simply for his own aggrandisement. Orwell also pointed out during the 1930s how the statistics issued by the U.S.S.R. were misleading and contradictory and when in 1941 many people were praising the cleverness of Stalin's foreign policy and the way that he kept shifting his attitude towards Germany, Orwell condemned it as treacherous and opportunistic. Nor would he silence his criticisms when the Soviet Union entered the Second World War on the side of the Allies. This was precisely the moment when he wrote *Animal Farm*.

In this novel Orwell reveals a simple, obvious and yet most profound observation about government: that dictators are the same, whether they come to power in a communist or a fascist country. Napoleon in *Animal Farm*, like Stalin and Hitler and all other dictators, establishes a personal life-style which must be supported by everything else in the community. Every part of national life becomes a matter of state, making the dictator's hold over his people more secure and his personal life more pleasant; the state becomes no more than the extension of his own vanity and he controls and absorbs the energies of the people by keeping the country mobilised as if for perpetual and total war. This is the inevitable end of the totalitarian state, the country where only one narrow set of beliefs is tolerated. Orwell thus revealed the psychological sameness of communism and fascism and did not shrink from criticising the abuse of socialism whilst remaining firmly committed to the socialist solution to the problems of the world.

The historical events behind Animal Farm

Animal Farm is a novel that can be responded to in different ways. On one level it is a wryly humorous animal story, a fable which reveals human weaknesses and strengths by seeing those characteristics acted out by animals. On another level it is an analysis of how and why revolutions fail and how power corrupts. But perhaps the most direct way of responding to *Animal Farm* is to see it as a satire on the events of the Russian Revolution and the rise of Russian communism. Orwell translates the events of Russian history between 1917 and 1943 into a delightfully controlled fantasy about the actions of animals on an English farm. To appreciate this satire and many of the details of the story, we need to know what happened in Russia during those years.

The Russian Revolution occurred in 1917. The people rose under the leadership of various revolutionary associations, the Tsar (or Emperor), Nicholas II, was deposed and eventually assassinated and his bureaucratic government was toppled. The revolution happened at this particular moment for two main reasons. Firstly, Marxist ideas had, since the end of the nineteenth century, been spreading amongst the middle classes and oppressed peasants of Russia. Secondly, Russia had entered the First World War in 1914 on the side of the Allies against Germany and had been badly weakened by the war. It was a good moment for a popular uprising to overthrow a government that had already lost its strength.

In 1918, the Bolsheviks emerged as the strongest of the revolutionary parties and took power by force. They were led by Lenin, who established 'the dictatorship of the common man', that is, rule by a small group of inner party members. Lenin was a hard realist and not a rigid doctrinaire communist and he allowed some private enterprise to continue. His economic policy was successful and it enabled Russia to recover from the years of dreadful famine after 1914. When he died in 1924 he had become a great national hero and his body was preserved in state in the Lenin Mausoleum in Moscow.

During the next three years there was a struggle for power between Stalin and Trotsky. It was not a mere personal struggle between two men of different temperaments but involved important differences of policy. Stalin wished to build communism in Russia first before attempting to achieve world revolution, while Trotsky regarded the world communist revolution as the great and urgent need. Stalin won the battle for power and eventually, in 1927, Trotsky was exiled and for the rest of his life he was constantly being accused of plotting against the Stalinist regime. He was finally assassinated in 1940 in Mexico.

Stalin swiftly developed an effective propaganda system, controlling all media outlets, and also a powerful secret police. He eliminated any possible rivals to his power and pressed millions of men into forced labour, on the excuse that they would not conform to his laws. He also replaced Lenin's mixed economy with more rigorous socialisation plans and continued the policy of Five Year Plans. These were major strategies for the economic improvement and industrialisation of the country, the first plan being proposed and outlined by Trotsky. Unfortunately, when it was implemented in 1928 it caused enormous hardship and famine in which five million peasants died. There was even a period of civil war in the Ukraine, where the kulaks (the richer, land-owning peasants) murdered the communist agents and deliberately destroyed crops and farm buildings.

Meanwhile, by the 1930s, Russia started entering into trade relations with the rest of Europe and even with the United States while the superior party officials, now established in power by the secret police, began to enjoy privileges and material comforts denied to ordinary men. Throughout this period, Stalin was developing the mystique of his own increasingly remote style of leadership, becoming an almost god-like and worshipped figure.

Stalin's foreign policy was firmly to oppose Nazism and he continued to denounce Hitler as an aggressor up to the spring of 1939. He entered into negotiations with Britain and France in order to form a mutual alliance against Nazi Germany. Yet, quite suddenly and without warning, in the summer of 1939 Stalin announced the signing of a non-aggression pact with Germany. He attempted in this way to force the best possible terms of alliance from either side, but the venture failed, for Hitler was as treacherous as Stalin and the Nazis invaded Russia in 1941 and destroyed much of the industrial and economic achievements of the previous decades before being driven back. This struggle to repel the invading Germans continued in Russia for two years, at an enormous cost in men and materials, neither side winning decisively. It was this invasion which forced the Soviet Union into alliance with Britain and the United States. In December 1943, the leaders of the three countries, Stalin, Churchill and Roosevelt, met together at Teheran (Iran) to plan the future strategy of the war.

George Orwell wrote *Animal Farm* between November 1943 and February 1944. It too concludes with a meeting, between the leading pigs and the humans from neighbouring farms. As you read the novel, refer to the notes at the end of this book. They point out many, more detailed parallels between modern Russian history and the story of the animals.

Animal Farm *as fable*

Animal Farm is a profound commentary on one of the most influential political philosophies of modern times. It is also, and has been from the moment of its publication, a source of delight and pleasure to its readers, provoking smiles of amusement and feelings of sadness. It is a book which can be enjoyed simply as a thoroughly entertaining story and it is appreciated in this way by many people, including even quite young children. How can this be? What has enabled George Orwell to distill such a weighty background of thought and experience into such a charming and appealing tale? The answer lies in his subtle and warmly humorous use of the type of story that we know as 'the fable'.

A fable is a story which illustrates human nature, our passions, feelings, successes and especially our failures, by presenting them in terms of the lives of animals. Orwell, in *Animal Farm*, achieves a range of effects in this way. To begin with, tragedy and horror are not allowed to destroy the light tone of the animal story. For example, the Battle of the Cowshed remains surprisingly within the bounds of the fairy story when the stable lad whom Boxer thought he had killed is discovered to have been merely knocked out and temporarily unconscious, and the destructive attack on the farm led by Frederick is likewise balanced by the ludicrous episode of Napoleon's hangover. The most moving part of the book is the death of Boxer, faithful and trusting to the end. We never see him being forced to face the true reality of his situation and so the episode is sad, full of pathos, but not tragic. There is a serious note struck also in the confessions and executions of Chapter 7 but here the intensity is diminished by the ridiculous:

> two other sheep confessed to having murdered an old ram, an especially devoted follower of Napoleon, by chasing him round and round a bonfire when he was suffering from a cough.

This combination of high seriousness with humour creates the most characteristic tone of the book. Orwell clarifies his message at the very moment when he is entertaining us most. There is a good example in the first chapter which is largely concerned with old Major's great speech to the animals in which he preaches the Marxist theory of labour and of the ideal society. His speech winds up to its climax:

'...And among us animals let there be perfect unity, perfect comradeship in the struggle. All men are enemies. All animals are comrades.'

At this moment there was a tremendous uproar. While Major was speaking four large rats had crept out of their holes and were sitting on their hindquarters listening to him. The dogs had suddenly caught sight of them, and it was only by a swift dash for their holes that the rats saved their lives.

So Orwell shifts the tone from the seriousness of the philosophy to the farcical confusion that results from the dogs chasing the rats. It is funny because it is entirely predictable animal behaviour but it is also a criticism of an over-idealistic philosophy that fails to take account of instinctive urges and individual needs. 'All animals are comrades' is a ridiculous assertion as the ensuing incident proves. A little later Major insists that the animals take a vote to decide whether rats are comrades. The criticism of unrealistic methods of social control is reinforced but it is all done so gently that it conveys its point in the raising of a smile; 'there were only four dissentients, the three dogs and the cat, who was afterwards discovered to have voted on both sides.'

Finally, some comments by Orwell himself on the way he wrote. The closing words of his essay 'Why I Write' are:

...looking back through my work, I see that it is invariably where I lacked a *political* purpose that I wrote lifeless books and was betrayed into purple passages, sentences without meaning, decorative adjectives and humbug generally.

Animal Farm contains none of these faults; it is fresh, economically written and engaging throughout. It is both profoundly serious and delightfully light and it achieves this remarkable blend, as Orwell suggests, because of its *political* motivation.

Animal Farm was the first book in which I tried, with full consciousness of what I was doing, to fuse political purpose and artistic purpose into one whole.

He was entirely successful.

Animal Farm

CHAPTER 1

MR. JONES, of the Manor Farm, had locked the hen-houses for the night, but was too drunk to remember to shut the pop-holes. With the ring of light from his lantern dancing from side to side, he lurched across the yard, kicking off his boots at the back door, drew himself a last glass of beer from the barrel in the scullery, and made his way up to bed, where Mrs. Jones was already snoring.

As soon as the light in the bedroom went out there was a stirring and a fluttering all through the farm buildings. Word had gone round during the day that old Major, the prize Middle White boar, had had a strange dream on the previous night and wished to communicate it to the other animals. It had been agreed that they should all meet in the big barn as soon as Mr. Jones was safely out of the way. Old Major (so he was always called, though the name under which he had been exhibited was Willingdon Beauty) was so highly regarded on the farm that everyone was quite ready to lose an hour's sleep in order to hear what he had to say.

At one end of the big barn, on a sort of raised platform, Major was already ensconced on his bed of straw, under a lantern which hung from a beam. He was twelve years old and had lately grown rather stout, but he was still a majestic-looking pig, with a wise and benevolent appearance in spite of the fact that his tushes had never been cut. Before long the other animals began to arrive and make themselves comfortable after their different fashions. First came the three dogs, Bluebell, Jessie, and Pitcher, and then the pigs who settled down in the straw immediately in front of the platform. The hens perched themselves on the window-sills, the pigeons fluttered up to the rafters, the sheep and cows lay down behind the pigs and began to chew the cud. The two cart-horses, Boxer and Clover, came in together, walking very slowly and setting down their vast hairy hoofs with great care lest there should be some small animal concealed in the straw. Clover was a stout motherly mare approaching middle life, who had never quite got her figure back after her fourth foal. Boxer was an enormous beast, nearly eighteen hands high, and as strong as any two ordinary horses put together. A white stripe down his nose gave him a somewhat stupid appearance, and in fact he was not of first-rate intelligence, but he was universally respected for his steadiness of character and tremendous powers of work. After the horses came Muriel, the white goat, and Benjamin, the donkey. Benjamin was the oldest animal on the farm, and the worst tempered. He seldom talked, and when he did it was usually to make some cynical remark—for instance, he would say that God had given him a tail to keep the flies off, but that he would sooner have had no tail and no flies. Alone among the animals on the farm he never laughed. If asked why, he would say that he saw nothing to laugh at. Nevertheless, without openly admitting it, he was devoted to Boxer; the two of them usually spent their Sundays together in the small paddock beyond the orchard, grazing side by side and never speaking.

The two horses had just lain down when a brood of ducklings, which had lost their mother, filed into the barn, cheeping feebly and wandering from side to side to find some place where they would not be trodden on. Clover made a sort of wall round them with her great foreleg, and the ducklings nestled down inside it, and promptly fell asleep. At the last moment Mollie, the foolish, pretty white mare who drew Mr. Jones's trap, came mincing daintily in, chewing at a lump of sugar. She took a place near the front and began flirting her white mane, hoping to draw attention to the red ribbons it was plaited with. Last of all came the cat, who

2

looked round, as usual, for the warmest place, and finally squeezed herself in between Boxer and Clover; there she purred contentedly throughout Major's speech without listening to a word of what he was saying. IGNORANT

All the animals were now present except Moses, the tame raven, who slept on a perch behind the back door. When Major saw that they had all made themselves comfortable and were waiting attentively, he cleared his throat and began:

'Comrades, you have heard already about the strange dream that I had last night. But I will come to the dream later. I have something else to say first. I do not think, comrades, that I shall be with you for many months longer, and before I die I feel it my duty to pass on to you such wisdom as I have acquired. I have had a long life, I have had much time for thought as I lay alone in my stall, and I think I may say that I understand the nature of life on this earth as well as any animal now living. It is about this that I wish to speak to you.

'Now, comrades, what is the nature of this life of ours? Let us face it: our lives are miserable, laborious, and short. We are born, we are given just so much food as will keep the breath in our bodies, and those of us who are capable of it are forced to work to the last atom of our strength; and the very instant that our usefulness has come to an end we are slaughtered with hideous cruelty. No animal in England knows the meaning of happiness or leisure after he is a year old. No animal in England is free. The life of an animal is misery and slavery: that is the plain truth. REASON FOR REVOLUTION

'But is this simply part of the order of nature? Is it because this land of ours is so poor that it cannot afford a decent life to those who dwell upon it? No, comrades, a thousand times no! The soil of England is fertile, its climate is good, it is capable of affording food in abundance to an enormously greater number of animals than now inhabit it. This single farm of ours would support a dozen horses, twenty cows, hundreds of sheep—and all of them living in a comfort and a dignity that

POOR LIVING CONDITIONS

3

are now almost beyond our imagining. Why then do we continue in this miserable condition? Because nearly the whole of the produce of our labour is stolen from us by human beings. There, comrades, is the answer to all our problems. It is summed up in a single word—Man. Man is the only real enemy we have. Remove Man from the scene, and the root cause of hunger and overwork is abolished for ever.

COMMON ENEMY

'Man is the only creature that consumes without producing. He does not give milk, he does not lay eggs, he is too weak to pull the plough, he cannot run fast enough to catch rabbits. Yet he is lord of all the animals. He sets them to work, he gives back to them the bare minimum that will prevent them from starving, and the rest he keeps for himself. Our labour tills the soil, our dung fertilizes it, and yet there is not one of us that owns more than his bare skin. You cows that I see before me, how many thousands of gallons of milk have you given during this last year? And what has happened to that milk which should have been breeding up sturdy calves? Every drop of it has gone down the throats of our enemies. And you hens, how many eggs have you laid this year, and how many of those eggs ever hatched into chickens? The rest have all gone to market to bring in money for Jones and his men. And you, Clover, where are those four foals you bore, who should have been the support and pleasure of your old age? Each was sold at a year old—you will never see one of them again. In return for your four confinements and all your labour in the field, what have you ever had except your bare rations and a stall?

'And even the miserable lives we lead are not allowed to reach their natural span. For myself I do not grumble, for I am one of the lucky ones. I am twelve years old and have had over four hundred children. Such is the natural life of a pig. But no animal escapes the cruel knife in the end. You young porkers who are sitting in front of me, every one of you will scream your lives out at the block within a year. To that

4

* GOOD QUOTE *

horror we all must come—cows, pigs, hens, sheep, everyone. Even the horses and the dogs have no better fate. You, Boxer, the very day that those great muscles of yours lose their power, Jones will sell you to the knacker, who will cut your throat and boil you down for the fox-hounds. As for the dogs, when they grow old and toothless, Jones ties a brick round their necks and drowns them in the nearest pond.

'Is it not crystal clear, then, comrades, that all the evils of this life of ours spring from the tyranny of human beings? Only get rid of Man, and the produce of our labour would be our own. Almost overnight we could become rich and free. What then must we do? Why, work night and day, body and soul, for the overthrow of the human race! That is my message to you, comrades: Rebellion! I do not know when that Rebellion will come, it might be in a week or in a hundred years, but I know, as surely as I see this straw beneath my feet, that sooner or later justice will be done. Fix your eyes on that, comrades, throughout the short remainder of your lives! And above all, pass on this message of mine to those who come after you, so that future generations shall carry on the struggle until it is victorious.

'And remember, comrades, your resolution must never falter. No argument must lead you astray. Never listen when they tell you that Man and the animals have a common interest, that the prosperity of the one is the prosperity of the others. It is all lies. Man serves the interests of no creature except himself. And among us animals let there be perfect unity, perfect comradeship in the struggle. All men are enemies. All animals are comrades.'

At this moment there was a tremendous uproar. While Major was speaking four large rats had crept out of their holes and were sitting on their hindquarters listening to him. The dogs had suddenly caught sight of them, and it was only by a swift dash for their holes that the rats saved their lives. Major raised his trotter for silence.

* GREAT IRONY AFTER REBELLION.

'Comrades,' he said, 'here is a point that must be settled. The wild creatures, such as rats and rabbits—are they our friends or our enemies? Let us put it to the vote. I propose this question to the meeting: Are rats comrades?'

The vote was taken at once, and it was agreed by an overwhelming majority that rats were comrades. There were only four dissentients, the three dogs and the cat, who was afterwards discovered to have voted on both sides. Major continued:

'I have little more to say. I merely repeat, remember always your duty of enmity towards Man and all his ways. Whatever goes upon two legs, is an enemy. Whatever goes upon four legs, or has wings, is a friend. And remember also that in fighting against Man, we must not come to resemble him. Even when you have conquered him, do not adopt his vices. No animal must ever live in a house, or sleep in a bed, or wear clothes, or drink alcohol, or smoke tobacco, or touch money, or engage in trade. All the habits of Man are evil. And, above all, no animal must ever tyrannize over his own kind. Weak or strong, clever or simple, we are all brothers. No animal must ever kill any other animal. All animals are equal.

'And now, comrades, I will tell you about my dream of last night. I cannot describe that dream to you. It was a dream of the earth as it will be when Man has vanished. But it reminded me of something that I had long forgotten. Many years ago, when I was a little pig, my mother and the other sows used to sing an old song of which they knew only the tune and the first three words. I had known that tune in my infancy, but it had long since passed out of my mind. Last night, however, it came back to me in my dream. And what is more, the words of the song also came back—words, I am certain, which were sung by the animals of long ago and have been lost to memory for generations. I will sing you that song now, comrades. I am old and my voice is hoarse, but when I have taught you the tune, you can sing it better for yourselves. It is called "Beasts of England".'

6

Old Major cleared his throat and began to sing. As he had said, his voice was hoarse, but he sang well enough, and it was a stirring tune, something between 'Clementine' and 'La Cucuracha'. The words ran:

Beasts of England, beasts of Ireland,
Beasts of every land and clime,
Hearken to my joyful tidings
Of the golden future time.

Soon or late the day is coming,
Tyrant Man shall be o'erthrown,
And the fruitful fields of England
Shall be trod by beasts alone.

Rings shall vanish from our noses,
And the harness from our back,
Bit and spur shall rust forever,
Cruel whips no more shall crack.

Riches more than mind can picture,
Wheat and barley, oats and hay,
Clover, beans, and mangel-wurzels
Shall be ours upon that day.

Bright will shine the fields of England,
Purer shall its waters be,
Sweeter yet shall blow its breezes
On the day that sets us free.

For that day we all must labour,
Though we die before it break;
Cows and horses, geese and turkeys,
All must toil for freedom's sake.

7

Beasts of England, beasts of Ireland,
Beasts of every land and clime,
Hearken well and spread my tidings
Of the golden future time.

The singing of this song threw the animals into the wildest
excitement. Almost before Major had reached the end, they
had begun singing it for themselves. Even the stupidest of
them had already picked up the tune and a few of the words,
and as for the clever ones, such as the pigs and dogs, they had
the entire song by heart within a few minutes. And then, after
a few preliminary tries, the whole farm burst out into 'Beasts
of England' in tremendous unison. The cows lowed it, the
dogs whined it, the sheep bleated it, the horses whinnied it, the
ducks quacked it. They were so delighted with the song that
they sang it right through five times in succession, and might
have continued singing it all night if they had not been
interrupted.

Unfortunately, the uproar awoke Mr. Jones, who sprang
out of bed, making sure that there was a fox in the yard. He
seized the gun which always stood in a corner of his bedroom,
and let fly a charge of number 6 shot into the darkness. The
pellets buried themselves in the wall of the barn and the
meeting broke up hurriedly. Everyone fled to his own sleeping place. The birds jumped on to their perches, the animals
settled down in the straw, and the whole farm was asleep in a
moment.

CHAPTER 2

THREE nights later old Major died peacefully in his sleep. His body was buried at the foot of the orchard.

This was early in March. During the next three months there was much secret activity. Major's speech had given to the more intelligent animals on the farm a completely new outlook on life. They did not know when the Rebellion predicted by Major would take place, they had no reason for thinking that it would be within their own lifetime, but they saw clearly that it was their duty to prepare for it. The work of teaching and organizing the others fell naturally upon the pigs, who were generally recognized as being the cleverest of the animals. Pre-eminent among the pigs were two young boars named Snowball and Napoleon, whom Mr. Jones was breeding up for sale. Napoleon was a large, rather fierce-looking Berkshire boar, the only Berkshire on the farm, not much of a talker, but with a reputation for getting his own way. Snowball was a more vivacious pig than Napoleon, quicker in speech and more inventive, but was not considered to have the same depth of character. All the other male pigs on the farm were porkers. The best known among them was a small fat pig named Squealer, with very round cheeks, twinkling eyes, nimble movements, and a shrill voice. He was a brilliant talker, and when he was arguing some difficult point he had a way of skipping from side to side and whisking his tail which was somehow very persuasive. The others said of Squealer that he could turn black into white.

These three had elaborated old Major's teachings into a complete system of thought, to which they gave the name of Animalism. Several nights a week, after Mr. Jones was asleep, they held secret meetings in the barn and expounded the principles of Animalism to the others. At the beginning they

9

met with much stupidity and apathy. Some of the animals talked of the duty of loyalty to Mr. Jones, whom they referred to as 'Master', or made elementary remarks such as 'Mr. Jones feeds us. If he were gone, we should starve to death.' Others asked such questions as 'Why should we care what happens after we are dead?' or 'If this rebellion is to happen anyway, what difference does it make whether we work for it or not?', and the pigs had great difficulty in making them see that this was contrary to the spirit of Animalism. The stupidest questions of all were asked by Mollie, the white mare. The very first question she asked Snowball was: 'Will there still be sugar after the Rebellion?'

'No,' said Snowball firmly. 'We have no means of making sugar on this farm. Besides, you do not need sugar. You will have all the oats and hay you want.'

'And shall I still be allowed to wear ribbons in my mane?' asked Mollie.

'Comrade,' said Snowball, 'those ribbons that you are so devoted to are the badge of slavery. Can you not understand that liberty is worth more than ribbons?'

Mollie agreed, but she did not sound very convinced.

The pigs had an even harder struggle to counteract the lies put about by Moses, the tame raven. Moses, who was Mr. Jones's especial pet, was a spy and a tale-bearer, but he was also a clever talker. He claimed to know the existence of a mysterious country called Sugarcandy Mountain, to which all animals went when they died. It was situated somewhere up in the sky, a little distance beyond the clouds, Moses said. In Sugarcandy Mountain it was Sunday seven days a week, clover was in season all the year round, and lump sugar and linseed cake grew on the hedges. The animals hated Moses because he told tales and did not work, but some of them believed in Sugarcandy Mountain, and the pigs had to argue very hard to persuade them that there was no such place.

Their most faithful disciples were the two cart-horses, Boxer

10

and Clover. These two had great difficulty in thinking any-thing out for themselves, but having once accepted the pigs as their teachers, they absorbed everything that they were told, and passed it on to the other animals by simple arguments. They were unfailing in their attendance at the secret meetings in the barn, and led the singing of 'Beasts of England', with which the meetings always ended.

Now, as it turned out, the Rebellion was achieved much earlier and more easily than anyone had expected. In past years Mr. Jones, although a hard master, had been a capable farmer, but of late he had fallen on evil days. He had become much disheartened after losing money in a lawsuit, and had taken to drinking more than was good for him. For whole days at a time he would lounge in his Windsor chair in the kitchen, reading the newspapers, drinking, and occasionally feeding Moses on crusts of bread soaked in beer. His men were idle and dishonest, the fields were full of weeds, the buildings wanted roofing, the hedges were neglected, and the animals were underfed.

June came and the hay was almost ready for cutting. On Midsummer's Eve, which was a Saturday, Mr. Jones went into Willingdon and got so drunk at the Red Lion that he did not come back till midday on Sunday. The men had milked the cows in the early morning and then had gone out rabbiting, without bothering to feed the animals. When Mr. Jones got back he immediately went to sleep on the drawing-room sofa with the *News of the World* over his face, so that when evening came, the animals were still unfed. At last they could stand it no longer. One of the cows broke in the door of the store-shed with her horns and all the animals began to help themselves from the bins. It was just then that Mr. Jones woke up. The next moment he and his four men were in the store-shed with whips in their hands, lashing out in all direc-tions. This was more than the hungry animals could bear. With one accord, though nothing of the kind had been planned beforehand, they flung themselves upon their tormentors. Jones and his men suddenly found themselves being butted and kicked from all sides. The situation was quite out of their control. They had never seen animals behave like this before, and this sudden uprising of creatures whom they were used to thrashing and maltreating just as they chose, frightened them almost out of their wits. After only a moment or two they gave up trying to defend themselves and took to their heels. A minute later all five of them were in full flight down the cart-track that led to the main road, with the animals pursuing them in triumph.

Mrs. Jones looked out of the bedroom window, saw what was happening, hurriedly flung a few possessions into a carpet bag, and slipped out of the farm by another way. Moses sprang off his perch and flapped after her, croaking loudly. Meanwhile the animals had chased Jones and his men out on to the road and slammed the five-barred gate behind them. And so, almost before they knew what was happening, the Rebellion had been successfully carried through: Jones was expelled, and the Manor Farm was theirs.

For the first few minutes the animals could hardly believe in their good fortune. Their first act was to gallop in a body right round the boundaries of the farm, as though to make quite sure that no human being was hiding anywhere upon it; then they raced back to the farm buildings to wipe out the last traces of Jones's hated reign. The harness-room at the end of the stables was broken open; the bits, the nose-rings, the dog-chains, the cruel knives with which Mr. Jones had been used to castrate the pigs and lambs, were all flung down the well. The reins, the halters, the blinkers, the degrading nosebags, were thrown on to the rubbish fire which was burning in the yard. So were the whips. All the animals capered with joy when they saw the whips going up in flames. Snowball also threw on to the fire the ribbons with which the horses' manes and tails had usually been decorated on market days.

'Ribbons,' he said, 'should be considered as clothes, which are the mark of a human being. All animals should go naked.'

When Boxer heard this he fetched the small straw hat which he wore in summer to keep the flies out of his ears, and flung it on to the fire with the rest.

In a very little while the animals had destroyed everything that reminded them of Mr. Jones. Napoleon then led them back to the store-shed and served out a double ration of corn to everybody, with two biscuits for each dog. Then they sang 'Beasts of England' from end to end seven times running, and after that they settled down for the night and slept as they had never slept before.

But they woke at dawn as usual, and suddenly remembering the glorious thing that had happened, they all raced out into the pasture together. A little way down the pasture there was a knoll that commanded a view of most of the farm. The animals rushed to the top of it and gazed round them in the clear morning light. Yes, it was theirs—everything that they could see was theirs! In the ecstasy of that thought they gambolled round and round, they hurled themselves into the air in great leaps of excitement. They rolled in the dew, they cropped mouthfuls of the sweet summer grass, they kicked up clods of the black earth and snuffed its rich scent. Then they made a tour of inspection of the whole farm and surveyed with speechless admiration the ploughland, the hayfield, the orchard, the pool, the spinney. It was as though they had never seen these things before, and even now they could hardly believe that it was all their own.

Then they filed back to the farm buildings and halted in silence outside the door of the farmhouse. That was theirs too, but they were frightened to go inside. After a moment, however, Snowball and Napoleon butted the door open with their shoulders and the animals entered in single file, walking with the utmost care for fear of disturbing anything. They tiptoed from room to room, afraid to speak above a whisper

13

and gazing with a kind of awe at the unbelievable luxury, at the beds with their feather mattresses, the looking-glasses, the horsehair sofa, the Brussels carpet, the lithograph of Queen Victoria over the drawing-room mantelpiece. They were just coming down the stairs when Mollie was discovered to be missing. Going back, the others found that she had remained behind in the best bedroom. She had taken a piece of blue ribbon from Mrs. Jones's dressing-table, and was holding it against her shoulder and admiring herself in the glass in a very foolish manner. The others reproached her sharply, and they went outside. Some hams hanging in the kitchen were taken out for burial, and the barrel of beer in the scullery was stove in with a kick from Boxer's hoof, otherwise nothing in the house was touched. A unanimous resolution was passed on the spot that the farmhouse should be preserved as a museum. All were agreed that no animal must ever live there. ⟶ IRONY LATER

The animals had their breakfast, and then Snowball and Napoleon called them together again.

'Comrades,' said Snowball, 'it is half past six and we have a long day before us. To-day we begin the hay harvest. But there is another matter that must be attended to first.'

The pigs now revealed that during the past three months they had taught themselves to read and write from an old spelling book which had belonged to Mr. Jones's children and which had been thrown on the rubbish heap. Napoleon sent for pots of black and white paint and led the way down to the five-barred gate that gave on to the main road. Then Snowball (for it was Snowball who was best at writing) took a brush between the two knuckles of his trotter, painted out MANOR FARM from the top bar of the gate and in its place painted ANIMAL FARM. This was to be the name of the farm from now onwards. After this they went back to the farm buildings, where Snowball and Napoleon sent for a ladder which they caused to be set against the end wall of the big barn. They explained that by their studies of the past three

14

months the pigs had succeeded in reducing the principles of Animalism to Seven Commandments. These Seven Commandments would now be inscribed on the wall; they would form an unalterable law by which all the animals on Animal Farm must live for ever after. With some difficulty (for it is not easy for a pig to balance himself on a ladder) Snowball climbed up and set to work, with Squealer a few rungs below him holding the paint-pot. The Commandments were written on the tarred wall in great white letters that could be read thirty yards away. They ran thus:

THE SEVEN COMMANDMENTS   PRINCIPLES OF ANIMALISM

1. *Whatever goes upon two legs is an enemy.*
2. *Whatever goes upon four legs, or has wings, is a friend.*
3. *No animal shall wear clothes.*
4. *No animal shall sleep in a bed.*
5. *No animal shall drink alcohol.*
6. *No animal shall kill any other animal.*
7. *All animals are equal.*

It was very neatly written, and except that 'friend' was written 'freind' and one of the 'S's' was the wrong way round, the spelling was correct all the way through. Snowball read it aloud for the benefit of the others. All the animals nodded in complete agreement, and the cleverer ones at once began to learn the Commandments by heart.

'Now, comrades,' said Snowball, throwing down the paint-brush, 'to the hayfield! Let us make it a point of honour to get in the harvest more quickly than Jones and his men could do.'

But at this moment the three cows, who had seemed uneasy for some time past, set up a loud lowing. They had not been milked for twenty-four hours, and their udders were almost bursting. After a little thought, the pigs sent for buckets and milked the cows fairly successfully, their trotters being well adapted to this task. Soon there were five buckets of frothing creamy milk at which many of the animals looked with considerable interest.

'What is going to happen to all that milk?' said someone.

'Jones used sometimes to mix some of it in our mash,' said one of the hens.

'Never mind the milk, comrades,' cried Napoleon, placing himself in front of the buckets. 'That will be attended to. The harvest is more important. Comrade Snowball will lead the way. I shall follow in a few minutes. Forward, comrades! The hay is waiting.'

So the animals trooped down to the hayfield to begin the harvest, and when they came back in the evening it was noticed that the milk had disappeared.

CORRUPTION ALREADY BY THE PIGS.

CHAPTER 3

How they toiled and sweated to get the hay in! But their efforts were rewarded, for the harvest was an even bigger success than they had hoped.

Sometimes the work was hard; the implements had been designed for human beings and not for animals, and it was a great drawback that no animal was able to use any tool that involved standing on his hind legs. But the pigs were so clever that they could think of a way round every difficulty. As for the horses, they knew every inch of the field, and in fact understood the business of mowing and raking far better than Jones and his men had ever done. The pigs did not actually work, but directed and supervised the others. With their superior knowledge it was natural that they should assume the leadership. Boxer and Clover would harness themselves to the cutter or the horse-rake (no bits or reins were needed in these days, of course) and tramp steadily round and round the field with a pig walking behind and calling out 'Gee up, comrade!' or 'Whoa back, comrade!' as the case might be. And every animal down to the humblest worked at turning the hay and gathering it. Even the ducks and hens toiled to and fro all day in the sun, carrying tiny wisps of hay in their beaks. In the end they finished the harvest in two days' less time than it had usually taken Jones and his men. Moreover, it was the biggest harvest that the farm had ever seen. There was no wastage whatever; the hens and ducks with their sharp eyes had gathered up the very last stalk. And not an animal on the farm had stolen so much as a mouthful.

All through that summer the work of the farm went like clockwork. The animals were happy as they had never conceived it possible to be. Every mouthful of food was an acute positive pleasure, now that it was truly their own food, produced by themselves and for themselves, not doled out to them by a grudging master. With the worthless parasitical human beings gone, there was more for everyone to eat. There was more leisure, too, inexperienced though the animals were. They met with many difficulties—for instance, later in the year, when they harvested the corn, they had to tread it out in the ancient style and blow away the chaff with their breath, since the farm possessed no threshing machine—but the pigs with their cleverness and Boxer with his tremendous muscles always pulled them through. Boxer was the admiration of everybody. He had been a hard worker even in Jones's time, but now he seemed more like three horses than one; there were days when the entire work of the farm seemed to rest upon his mighty shoulders. From morning to night he was pushing and pulling, always at the spot where the work was hardest. He had made an arrangement with one of the cockerels to call him in the mornings half an hour earlier than anyone else, and would put in some volunteer labour at whatever seemed to be most needed, before the regular day's work began. His answer to every problem, every setback, was 'I will work harder!'— which he had adopted as his personal motto.

But everyone worked according to his capacity. The hens and ducks, for instance, saved five bushels of corn at the harvest by gathering up the stray grains. Nobody stole, nobody grumbled over his rations, the quarrelling and biting and jealousy which had been normal features of life in the old days had almost disappeared. Nobody shirked—or almost nobody. Mollie, it was true, was not good at getting up in the morning, and had a way of leaving work early on the ground that there was a stone in her hoof. And the behaviour of the cat was somewhat peculiar. It was soon noticed that when there was work to be done the cat could never be found. She would vanish for hours on end, and then reappear at meal-times, or in the evening after work was over, as though nothing had happened. But she always made such excellent excuses, and purred so affectionately, that it was impossible not to believe in her good intentions. Old Benjamin, the donkey, seemed quite unchanged since the Rebellion. He did his work in the same slow obstinate way as he had done it in Jones's time, never shirking, and never volunteering for extra work either. About the Rebellion and its results he would express no opinion. When asked whether he was not happier now that Jones was gone, he would say only 'Donkeys live a long time. None of you has ever seen a dead donkey,' and the others had to be content with this cryptic answer.

On Sundays there was no work. Breakfast was an hour later than usual, and after breakfast there was a ceremony which was observed every week without fail. First came the hoisting of the flag. Snowball had found in the harness-room an old green tablecloth of Mrs. Jones's, and had painted on it a hoof and a horn in white. This was run up the flagstaff in the farmhouse garden every Sunday morning. The flag was green, Snowball explained, to represent the green fields of England, while the hoof and horn signified the future Republic of the

Animals which would arise when the human race had been finally overthrown. After the hoisting of the flag all the animals trooped into the big barn for a general assembly which was known as the Meeting. Here the work of the coming week was planned out and resolutions were put forward and debated. It was always the pigs who put forward the resolutions. The other animals understood how to vote, but could never think of any resolutions of their own. Snowball and Napoleon were by far the most active in the debates. But it was noticed that these two were never in agreement: whatever suggestion either of them made, the other could be counted on to oppose it. Even when it was resolved—a thing no one could object to in itself—to set aside a small paddock behind the orchard as a home of rest for animals who were past work, there was a stormy debate over the correct retiring age for each class of animal. The Meeting always ended with the singing of 'Beasts of England', and the afternoon was given up to recreation.

The pigs had set aside the harness-room as a headquarters for themselves. Here, in the evening, they studied blacksmithing, carpentering, and other necessary arts from books which they had brought out of the farmhouse. Snowball also busied himself with organizing the other animals into what he called Animal Committees. He was indefatigable at this. He formed the Egg Production Committee for the hens, the Clean Tails League for the cows, the Wild Comrades' Re-education Committee (the object of this was to tame the rats and rabbits), the Whiter Wool Movement for the sheep, and various others, besides instituting classes in reading and writing. On the whole, these projects were a failure. The attempt to tame the wild creatures, for instance, broke down almost immediately. They continued to behave very much as before, and when treated with generosity, simply took advantage of it. The cat joined the Re-education Committee and was very active in it for some days. She was seen one day sitting on a roof and talking to some sparrows who were just out of her reach. She was telling them that all animals were now comrades and that any sparrow who chose could come and perch on her paw; but the sparrows kept their distance. The reading and writing classes, however, were a great success. By the autumn almost every animal on the farm was literate in some degree.

As for the pigs, they could already read and write perfectly. The dogs learned to read fairly well, but were not interested in reading anything except the Seven Commandments. Muriel, the goat, could read somewhat better than the dogs, and sometimes used to read to the others in the evenings from scraps of newspaper which she found on the rubbish heap. Benjamin could read as well as any pig, but never exercised his faculty. So far as he knew, he said, there was nothing worth reading. Clover learnt the whole alphabet, but could not put words together. Boxer could not get beyond the letter D. He would trace out A, B, C, D, in the dust with his great hoof, and then would stand staring at the letters with his ears back, sometimes shaking his forelock, trying with all his might to remember what came next and never succeeding. On several occasions, indeed, he did learn E, F. G, H, but by the time he knew them, it was always discovered that he had forgotten A, B, C, and D. Finally he decided to be content with the first four letters, and used to write them out once or twice every day to refresh his memory. Mollie refused to learn any but the six letters which spelt her own name. She would form these very neatly out of pieces of twig, and would then decorate them with a flower or two and walk round them admiring them.

None of the other animals on the farm could get further than the letter A. It was also found that the stupider animals, such as the sheep, hens, and ducks, were unable to learn the Seven Commandments by heart. After much thought Snowball declared that the Seven Commandments could in effect be reduced to a single maxim, namely: 'Four legs good, two legs bad.' This, he said, contained the essential principle of

Animalism. Whoever had thoroughly grasped it would be safe from human influences. The birds at first objected, since it seemed to them that they also had two legs, but Snowball proved to them that this was not so.

'A bird's wing, comrades,' he said, 'is an organ of propulsion and not of manipulation. It should therefore be regarded as a leg. The distinguishing mark of Man is the *hand*, the instrument with which he does all his mischief.'

The birds did not understand Snowball's long words, but they accepted his explanation, and all the humbler animals set to work to learn the new maxim by heart. FOUR LEGS GOOD, TWO LEGS BAD, was inscribed on the end wall of the barn, above the Seven Commandments and in bigger letters. When they had once got it by heart, the sheep developed a great liking for this maxim, and often as they lay in the field they would all start bleating 'Four legs good, two legs bad! Four legs good, two legs bad!' and kept it up for hours on end, never growing tired of it.

Napoleon took no interest in Snowball's committees. He said that the education of the young was more important than anything that could be done for those who were already grown up. It happened that Jessie and Bluebell had both whelped soon after the hay harvest, giving birth between them to nine sturdy puppies. As soon as they were weaned, Napoleon took them away from their mothers, saying that he would make himself reponsible for their education. He took them up into a loft which could only be reached by a ladder from the harness-room, and there kept them in such seclusion that the rest of the farm soon forgot their existence.

The mystery of where the milk went to was soon cleared up. It was mixed every day into the pigs' mash. The early apples were now ripening, and the grass of the orchard was littered with windfalls. The animals had assumed as a matter of course that these would be shared out equally; one day, however, the order went forth that all the windfalls were to be collected and brought to the harness-room for the use of the pigs. At this some of the other animals murmured, but it was no use. All the pigs were in full agreement on this point, even Snowball and Napoleon. Squealer was sent to make the necessary explanation to the others.

'Comrades!' he cried. 'You do not imagine, I hope, that we pigs are doing this in a spirit of selfishness and privilege? Many of us actually dislike milk and apples. I dislike them myself. Our sole object in taking these things is to preserve our health. Milk and apples (this has been proved by Science, comrades) contain substances absolutely necessary to the well-being of a pig. We pigs are brain-workers. The whole management and organization of this farm depend on us. Day and night we are watching over your welfare. It is for *your* sake that we drink that milk and eat those apples. Do you know what would happen if we pigs failed in our duty? Jones would come back! Yes, Jones would come back! Surely, comrades,' cried Squealer almost pleadingly, skipping from side to side and whisking his tail, 'surely there is no one among you who wants to see Jones come back?'

Now if there was one thing that the animals were completely certain of, it was that they did not want Jones back. When it was put to them in this light, they had no more to say. The importance of keeping the pigs in good health was all too obvious. So it was agreed without further argument that the milk and the windfall apples (and also the main crop of apples when they ripened) should be reserved for the pigs alone.

CHAPTER 4

By the late summer the news of what had happened on Animal Farm had spread across half the country. Every day Snowball and Napoleon sent out flights of pigeons whose instructions were to mingle with the animals on neighbouring farms, tell them the story of the Rebellion, and teach them the tune of 'Beasts of England'.

Most of this time Mr. Jones had spent sitting in the tap-room of the Red Lion at Willingdon, complaining to anyone who would listen of the monstrous injustice he had suffered in being turned out of his property by a pack of good-for-nothing animals. The other farmers sympathized in principle, but they did not at first give him much help. At heart, each of them was secretly wondering whether he could not somehow turn Jones's misfortune to his own advantage. It was lucky that the owners of the two farms which adjoined Animal Farm were on permanently bad terms. One of them, which was named Foxwood, was a large, neglected, old-fashioned farm, much overgrown by woodland, with all its pastures worn out and its hedges in a disgraceful condition. Its owner, Mr. Pilkington, was an easy-going gentleman farmer who spent most of his time in fishing or hunting according to the season. The other farm, which was called Pinchfield, was smaller and better kept. Its owner was a Mr. Frederick, a tough, shrewd man, perpetually involved in lawsuits and with a name for driving hard bargains. These two disliked each other so much that it was difficult for them to come to any agreement, even in defence of their own interests.

Nevertheless, they were both thoroughly frightened by the rebellion on Animal Farm, and very anxious to prevent their own animals from learning too much about it. At first they pretended to laugh to scorn the idea of animals managing a farm for themselves. The whole thing would be over in a fortnight, they said. They put it about that the animals on the Manor Farm (they insisted on calling it the Manor Farm; they would not tolerate the name 'Animal Farm') were perpetually fighting among themselves and were also rapidly starving to death. When time passed and the animals had evidently not starved to death, Frederick and Pilkington changed their tune and began to talk of the terrible wickedness that now flourished on Animal Farm. It was given out that the animals there practised cannibalism, tortured one another with red-hot horseshoes, and had their females in common. This was what came of rebelling against the laws of Nature, Frederick and Pilkington said.

However, these, stories were never fully believed. Rumours of a wonderful farm, where the human beings had been turned out and the animals managed their own affairs, continued to circulate in vague and distorted forms, and throughout that year a wave of rebelliousness ran through the countryside. Bulls which had always been tractable suddenly turned savage, sheep broke down hedges and devoured the clover, cows kicked the pail over, hunters refused their fences and shot their riders on to the other side. Above all, the tune and even the words of 'Beasts of England' were known everywhere. It had spread with astonishing speed. The human beings could not contain their rage when they heard this song, though they pretended to think it merely ridiculous. They could not understand, they said, how even animals could bring themselves to sing such contemptible rubbish. Any animal caught singing it was given a flogging on the spot. And yet the song was irrepressible. The blackbirds whistled it in the hedges, the pigeons cooed it in the elms, it got into the din of the smithies and the tune of the church bells. And when the human beings listened to it, they secretly trembled, hearing in it a prophecy of their future doom.

Early in October, when the corn was cut and stacked and

some of it was already threshed, a flight of pigeons came whirling through the air and alighted in the yard of Animal Farm in the wildest excitement. Jones and all his men, with half a dozen others from Foxwood and Pinchfield, had entered the five-barred gate and were coming up the cart-track that led to the farm. They were all carrying sticks, except Jones, who was marching ahead with a gun in his hands. Obviously they were going to attempt the recapture of the farm.

This had long been expected, and all preparations had been made. Snowball, who had studied an old book of Julius Caesar's campaigns which he had found in the farmhouse, was in charge of the defensive operations. He gave his orders quickly, and in a couple of minutes every animal was at his post.

As the human beings approached the farm buildings, Snowball launched his first attack. All the pigeons, to the number of thirty-five, flew to and fro over the men's head and muted upon them from mid-air; and while the men were dealing with this, the geese, who had been hiding behind the hedge, rushed out and pecked viciously at the calves of their legs. However, this was only a light skirmishing manoeuvre, intended to create a little disorder, and the men easily drove the geese off with their sticks. Snowball now launched his second line of attack. Muriel, Benjamin, and all the sheep, with Snowball at the head of them, rushed forward and prodded and butted the men from every side, while Benjamin turned round and lashed at them with his small hoofs. But once again the men, with their sticks and their hobnailed boots, were too strong for them; and suddenly, at a squeal from Snowball, which was the signal for retreat, all the animals turned and fled through the gateway into the yard.

The men gave a shout of triumph. They saw, as they imagined, their enemies in flight, and they rushed after them in disorder. This was just what Snowball had intended. As soon as they were well inside the yard, the three horses, the three cows, and the rest of the pigs, who had been lying in ambush in the cowshed, suddenly emerged in their rear, cutting them off. Snowball now gave the signal for the charge. He himself dashed straight for Jones. Jones saw him coming, raised his gun, and fired. The pellets scored bloody streaks along Snowball's back, and a sheep dropped dead. Without halting for an instant Snowball flung his fifteen stone against Jones's legs. Jones was hurled into a pile of dung and his gun flew out of his hands. But the most terrifying spectacle of all was Boxer, rearing up on his hind legs and striking out with his great iron-shod hoofs like a stallion. His very first blow took a stable-lad from Foxwood on the skull and stretched him lifeless in the mud. At the sight, several men dropped their sticks and tried to run. Panic overtook them, and the next moment all the animals together were chasing them round and round the yard. They were gored, kicked, bitten, trampled on. There was not an animal on the farm that did not take vengeance on them after his own fashion. Even the cat suddenly leapt off a roof on to a cowman's shoulders and sank her claws in his neck, at which he yelled horribly. At a moment when the opening was clear, the men were glad enough to rush out of the yard and make a bolt for the main road. And so within five minutes of their invasion they were in ignominious retreat by the same way as they had come, with a flock of geese hissing after them and pecking at their calves all the way.

All the men were gone except one. Back in the yard Boxer was pawing with his hoof at the stable-lad who lay face down in the mud, trying to turn him over. The boy did not stir.

'He is dead,' said Boxer sorrowfully. 'I had no intention of doing that. I forgot that I was wearing iron shoes. Who will believe that I did not do this on purpose?'

'No sentimentality, comrade!' cried Snowball, from whose

wounds the blood was still dripping. 'War is war. The only good human being is a dead one.'

'I have no wish to take life, not even human life,' repeated Boxer, and his eyes were full of tears.

'Where is Mollie?' exclaimed somebody.

Mollie in fact was missing. For a moment there was great alarm; it was feared that the men might have harmed her in some way, or even carried her off with them. In the end, however, she was found hiding in her stall with her head buried among the hay in the manger. She had taken flight as soon as the gun went off. And when the others came back from looking for her, it was to find that the stable-lad, who in fact was only stunned, had already recovered and made off.

The animals had now reassembled in the wildest excitement, each recounting his own exploits in the battle at the top of his voice. An impromptu celebration of the victory was held immediately. The flag was run up and 'Beasts of England' was sung a number of times, then the sheep who had been killed was given a solemn funeral, a hawthorn bush being planted on her grave. At the graveside Snowball made a little speech, emphasizing the need for all animals to be ready to die for Animal Farm if need be.

The animals decided unanimously to create a military decoration, 'Animal Hero, First Class', which was conferred there and then on Snowball and Boxer. It consisted of a brass medal (they were really some old horse-brasses which had been found in the harness-room), to be worn on Sundays and holidays. There was also 'Animal Hero, Second Class', which was conferred posthumously on the dead sheep.

There was much discussion as to what the battle should be called. In the end, it was named the Battle of the Cowshed, since that was where the ambush had been sprung. Mr. Jones's gun had been found lying in the mud, and it was known that there was a supply of cartridges in the farmhouse. It was

27

decided to set the gun up at the foot of the flagstaff, like a piece of artillery, and to fire it twice a year—once on October the twelfth, the anniversary of the Battle of the Cowshed, and once on Midsummer Day, the anniversary of the Rebellion.

CHAPTER 5

As winter drew on, Mollie became more and more troublesome. She was late for work every morning and excused herself by saying that she had overslept, and she complained of mysterious pains, although her appetite was excellent. On every kind of pretext she would run away from work and go to the drinking pool, where she would stand foolishly gazing at her own reflection in the water. But there were also rumours of something more serious. One day as Mollie strolled blithely into the yard, flirting her long tail and chewing at a stalk of hay, Clover took her aside.

'Mollie,' she said, 'I have something very serious to say to you. This morning I saw you looking over the hedge that divides Animal Farm from Foxwood. One of Mr. Pilkington's men was standing on the other side of the hedge. And—I was a long way away, but I am almost certain I saw this—he was talking to you and you were allowing him to stroke your nose. What does that mean, Mollie?'

'He didn't! I wasn't! It isn't true!' cried Mollie, beginning to prance about and paw the ground.

'Mollie! Look me in the face. Do you give me your word of honour that the man was not stroking your nose?'

'It isn't true!' repeated Mollie, but she could not look Clover in the face, and the next moment she took to her heels and galloped away into the field.

A thought struck Clover. Without saying anything to the

others, she went to Mollie's stall and turned over the straw with her hoof. Hidden under the straw was a little pile of lump sugar and several bunches of ribbon of different colours.

Three days later Mollie disappeared. For some weeks nothing was known of her whereabouts, then the pigeons reported that they had seen her on the other side of Willingdon. She was between the shafts of a smart dogcart painted red and black, which was standing outside a public-house. A fat red-faced man in check breeches and gaiters, who looked like a publican, was stroking her nose and feeding her with sugar. Her coat was newly clipped and she wore a scarlet ribbon round her forelock. She appeared to be enjoying herself, so the pigeons said. None of the animals ever mentioned Mollie again.

In January there came bitterly hard weather. The earth was like iron, and nothing could be done in the fields. Many meetings were held in the big barn, and the pigs occupied themselves in planning out the work of the coming season. It had come to be accepted that the pigs, who were manifestly cleverer than the other animals, should decide all questions of farm policy, though their decisions had to be ratified by a majority vote. This arrangement would have worked well enough if it had not been for the disputes between Snowball and Napoleon. These two disagreed at every point where disagreement was possible. If one of them suggested sowing a bigger acreage with barley, the other was certain to demand a bigger acreage of oats, and if one of them said that such and such a field was just right for cabbages, the other would declare that it was useless for anything except roots. Each had his own following, and there were some violent debates. At the Meetings Snowball often won over the majority by his brilliant speeches, but Napoleon was better at canvassing support for himself in between times. He was especially successful with the sheep. Of late the sheep had taken to bleating 'Four legs good, two legs bad' both in and out of season, and they often interrupted the Meeting with this. It was noticed that they were especially liable to break into 'Four legs good, two legs bad' at the crucial moments in Snowball's speeches. Snowball had made a close study of some back numbers of the *Farmer and Stockbreeder* which he had found in the farmhouse, and was full of plans for innovations and improvements. He talked learnedly about field-drains, silage, and basic slag, and had worked out a complicated scheme for all the animals to drop their dung directly in the fields, at a different spot every day, to save the labour of cartage. Napoleon produced no schemes of his own, but said quietly that Snowball's would come to nothing, and seemed to be biding his time. But of all their controversies, none was so bitter as the one that took place over the windmill.

In the long pasture, not far from the farm buildings, there was a small knoll which was the highest point on the farm. After surveying the ground, Snowball declared that this was just the place for a windmill, which could be made to operate a dynamo and supply the farm with electrical power. This would light the stalls and warm them in winter, and would also run a circular saw, a chaff-cutter, a mangel-slicer, and an electric milking machine. The animals had never heard of anything of this kind before (for the farm was an old-fashioned one and had only the most primitive machinery), and they listened in astonishment while Snowball conjured up pictures of fantastic machines which would do their work for them while they grazed at their ease in the fields or improved their minds with reading and conversation.

Within a few weeks Snowball's plan for the windmill were fully worked out. The mechanical details came mostly from three books which had belonged to Mr. Jones—*One Thousand Useful Things to Do About the House, Every Man His Own Bricklayer,* and *Electricity for Beginners.* Snowball used as his study a shed which had once been used for incubators and had a smooth wooden floor, suitable for drawing on. He was closeted there for hours at a time. With his books held open by a stone, and with a piece of chalk gripped between the knuckles of his trotter, he would move rapidly to and fro, drawing in line after line and uttering little whimpers of excitement. Gradually the plans grew into a complicated mass of cranks and cog-wheels, covering more than half the floor, which the other animals found completely unintelligible but very impressive. All of them came to look at Snowball's drawings at least once a day. Even the hens and ducks came, and were at pains not to tread on the chalk marks. Only Napoleon held aloof. He had declared himself against the windmill from the start. One day, however, he arrived unexpectedly to examine the plans. He walked heavily round the shed, looked closely at every detail of the plans and snuffed at them once or twice, then stood for a little while contemplating them out of the corner of his eye; then suddenly he lifted his leg, urinated over the plans, and walked out without uttering a word.

The whole farm was deeply divided on the subject of the windmill. Snowball did not deny that to build it would be a difficult business. Stone would have to be quarried and built up into walls, then the sails would have to be made and after that there would be need for dynamos and cables. (How these were to be procured, Snowball did not say.) But he maintained that it could all be done in a year. And thereafter, he declared, so much labour would be saved that the animals would only need to work three days a week. Napoleon, on the other hand, argued that the great need of the moment was to increase food production, and that if they wasted time on the windmill they would all starve to death. The animals formed themselves into two factions under the slogans, 'Vote for Snowball and the three-day week' and 'Vote for Napoleon and the full manger'. Benjamin was the only animal who did not side with either faction. He refused to believe either that food would become more plentiful or that the windmill would save work.

Windmill or no windmill, he said, life would go on as it had always gone on—that is, badly.

Apart from the disputes over the windmill, there was the question of the defence of the farm. It was fully realized that though the human beings had been defeated in the Battle of the Cowshed they might make another and more determined attempt to recapture the farm and reinstate Mr. Jones. They had all the more reason for doing so because the news of their defeat had spread across the countryside and made the animals on the neighbouring farms more restive than ever. As usual, Snowball and Napoleon were in disagreement. According to Napoleon, what the animals must do was to procure firearms and train themselves in the use of them. According to Snowball, they must send out more and more pigeons and stir up rebellion among the animals on the other farms. The one argued that if they could not defend themselves they were bound to be conquered, the other argued that if rebellions happened everywhere they would have no need to defend themselves. The animals listened first to Napoleon, then to Snowball, and could not make up their minds which was right; indeed, they always found themselves in agreement with the one who was speaking at the moment.

At last the day came when Snowball's plans were completed. At the Meeting on the following Sunday the question of whether or not to begin work on the windmill was to be put to the vote. When the animals had assembled in the big barn, Snowball stood up and, though occasionally interrupted by bleating from the sheep, set forth his reasons for advocating the building of the windmill. Then Napoleon stood up to reply. He said very quietly that the windmill was nonsense and that he advised nobody to vote for it, and promptly sat down again; he had spoken for barely thirty seconds, and seemed almost indifferent as to the effect he produced. At this Snowball sprang to his feet, and shouting down the sheep, who had begun bleating again, broke into a passionate appeal in favour of the windmill. Until now the animals had been about equally divided in their sympathies, but in a moment Snowball's eloquence had carried them away. In glowing sentences he painted a picture of Animal Farm as it might be when sordid labour was lifted from the animals' backs. His imagination had now run far beyond chaff-cutters and turnip-slicers. Electricity, he said, could operate threshing machines, ploughs, harrows, rollers and reapers and binders, besides supplying every stall with its own electric light, hot and cold water, and an electric heater. By the time he had finished speaking, there was no doubt as to which way the vote would go. But just at this moment Napoleon stood up and, casting a peculiar sidelong look at Snowball, uttered a high-pitched whimper of a kind no one had ever heard him utter before.

At this there was a terrible baying sound outside, and nine enormous dogs wearing brass-studded collars came bounding into the barn. They dashed straight for Snowball, who only sprang from his place just in time to escape their snapping jaws. In a moment he was out of the door and they were after him. Too amazed and frightened to speak, all the animals crowded through the door to watch the chase. Snowball was racing across the long pasture that led to the road. He was running as only a pig can run, but the dogs were close on his heels. Suddenly he slipped and it seemed certain that they had him. Then he was up again, running faster than ever, then the dogs were gaining on him again. One of them all but closed his jaws on Snowball's tail, but Snowball whisked it free just in time. Then he put on an extra spurt and, with a few inches to spare, slipped through a hole in the hedge and was seen no more.

Silent and terrified, the animals crept back into the barn. In a moment the dogs came bounding back. At first no one had been able to imagine where these creatures came from, but the problem was soon solved: they were the puppies whom Napoleon had taken away from their mothers and reared privately. Though not yet full-grown, they were huge dogs, and as fierce-looking as wolves. They kept close to Napoleon. It was noticed that they wagged their tails to him in the same way as the other dogs had been used to do to Mr. Jones.

Napoleon, with the dogs following him, now mounted on to the raised portion of the floor where Major had previously stood to deliver his speech. He announced that from now on the Sunday morning Meetings would come to an end. They were unnecessary, he said, and wasted time. In future all questions relating to the working of the farm would be settled by a special committee of pigs, presided over by himself. These would meet in private and afterwards communicate their decisions to the others. The animals would still assemble on Sunday mornings to salute the flag, sing 'Beasts of England', and receive their orders for the week; but there would be no more debates.

In spite of the shock that Snowball's expulsion had given them, the animals were dismayed by this announcement. Several of them would have protested if they could have found the right arguments. Even Boxer was vaguely troubled. He set his ears back, shook his forelock several times and tried hard to marshal his thoughts; but in the end he could not think of anything to say. Some of the pigs themselves, however, were more articulate. Four young porkers in the front row uttered shrill squeals of disapproval, and all four of them sprang to their feet and began speaking at once. But suddenly the dogs sitting round Napoleon let out deep, menacing growls, and the pigs fell silent and sat down again. Then the sheep broke out into a tremendous bleating of 'Four legs good, two legs bad!' which went on for nearly a quarter of an hour and put an end to any chance of discussion.

Afterwards Squealer was sent round the farm to explain the new arrangement to the others.

'Comrades,' he said, 'I trust that every animal here appreci-ates the sacrifice that Comrade Napoleon has made in taking this extra labour upon himself. Do not imagine, comrade, that leadership is a pleasure! On the contrary, it is a deep and heavy responsibility. No one believes more firmly than Comrade Napoleon that all animals are equal. He would be only too happy to let you make your decisions for yourselves. But sometimes you might make the wrong decisions, comrades, and then where should we be? Suppose you had decided to follow Snowball, with his moonshine of windmills—Snowball, who, as we now know, was no better than a criminal?'

'He fought bravely at the Battle of the Cowshed,' said somebody.

'Bravery is not enough,' said Squealer. 'Loyalty and obedience are more important. And as to the Battle of the Cowshed, I believe the time will come when we shall find that Snowball's part in it was much exaggerated. Discipline, comrades, iron discipline! That is the watchword for today. One false step, and our enemies would be upon us. Surely, comrades, you do not want Jones back?'

Once again this argument was unanswerable. Certainly the animals did not want Jones back; if the holding of debates on Sunday mornings was liable to bring him back, then the debates must stop. Boxer, who had now had time to think things over, voiced the general feeling by saying: 'If Comrade Napoleon says it, it must be right'. And from then on he adopted the maxim, 'Napoleon is always right,' in addition to his private motto of 'I will work harder.'

By this time the weather had broken and the spring ploughing had begun. The shed where Snowball had drawn his plans of the windmill had been shut up and it was assumed that the plans had been rubbed off the floor. Every Sunday morning at ten o'clock the animals assembled in the big barn to receive their orders for the week. The skull of old Major, now clean of flesh, had been disinterred from the orchard and set up on a stump at the foot of the flagstaff, beside the gun.

After the hoisting of the flag, the animals were required to file past the skull in a reverent manner before entering the barn. Nowadays they did not sit all together as they had done in the past. Napoleon, with Squealer and another pig named Minimus, who had a remarkable gift for composing songs and poems, sat on the front of the raised platform, with the nine young dogs forming a semicircle round them, and the other pigs sitting behind. The rest of the animals sat facing them in the main body of the barn. Napoleon read out the orders for the week in a gruff soldierly style, and after a single singing of 'Beasts of England', all the animals dispersed.

On the third Sunday after Snowball's expulsion, the animals were somewhat surprised to hear Napoleon announce that the windmill was to be built after all. He did not give any reasons for having changed his mind, but merely warned the animals that this extra task would mean very hard work; it might even be necessary to reduce their rations. The plans, however, had all been prepared, down to the last detail. A special committee of pigs had been at work upon them for the past three weeks. The building of the windmill, with various other improvements, was expected to take two years.

That evening Squealer explained privately to the other animals that Napoleon had never in reality been opposed to the windmill. On the contrary, it was he who had advocated it in the beginning, and the plan which Snowball had drawn on the floor of the incubator shed had actually been stolen from among Napoleon's papers. The windmill was, in fact, Napoleon's own creation. Why, then, asked somebody, had he spoken so strongly against it? Here Squealer looked very sly. That, he said, was Comrade Napoleon's cunning. He had *seemed* to oppose the windmill, simply as a manoeuvre to get rid of Snowball, who was a dangerous character and a bad influence. Now that Snowball was out of the way, the plan could go forward without his interference. This, said Squealer, was something called tactics. He repeated a number of times, 'Tactics, comrades, tactics!' skipping round and whisking his tail with a merry laugh. The animals were not certain what the word meant, but Squealer spoke so persuasively, and the three dogs who happened to be with him growled so threateningly, that they accepted his explanation without further questions.

CHAPTER 6

ALL that year the animals worked like slaves. But they were happy in their work; they grudged no effort or sacrifice, well aware that everything that they did was for the benefit of themselves and those of their kind who would come after them, and not for a pack of idle, thieving human beings.

Throughout the spring and summer they worked a sixty-hour week, and in August Napoleon announced that there would be work on Sunday afternoons as well. This work was strictly voluntary, but any animal who absented himself from it would have his rations reduced by half. Even so, it was found necessary to leave certain tasks undone. The harvest was a little less successful than in the previous year, and two fields which should have been sown with roots in the early summer were not sown because the ploughing had not been completed early enough. It was possible to foresee that the coming winter would be a hard one.

The windmill presented unexpected difficulties. There was a good quarry of limestone on the farm, and plenty of sand and cement had been found in one of the outhouses, so that all the materials for building were at hand. But the problem the animals could not at first solve was how to break up the stones into pieces of suitable size. There seemed no way of doing this except with picks and crowbars, which no animal could use, because no animal could stand on his hind legs. Only after weeks of vain effort did the right idea occur to some-body—namely, to utilize the force of gravity. Huge boulders, far too big to be used as they were, were lying all over the bed of the quarry. The animals lashed ropes round these, and then all together, cows, horses, sheep, any animal that could lay hold of the rope—even the pigs sometimes joined in at critical moments—they dragged them with desperate slowness up the slope to the top of the quarry, where they were toppled over the edge, to shatter to pieces below. Transporting the stone when it was once broken was comparatively simple. The horses carried it off in cart-loads, the sheep dragged single blocks, even Muriel and Benjamin yoked themselves into an old governess-cart and did their share. By late summer a sufficient store of stone had accumulated, and then the build-ing began, under the superintendence of the pigs.

But it was a slow, laborious process. Frequently it took a whole day of exhausting effort to drag a single boulder to the top of the quarry, and sometimes when it was pushed over the edge it failed to break. Nothing could have been achieved without Boxer, whose strength seemed equal to that of all the rest of the animals put together. When the boulder began to slip and the animals cried out in despair at finding themselves dragged down the hill, it was always Boxer who strained him-self against the rope and brought the boulder to a stop. To see him toiling up the slope inch by inch, his breath coming fast, the tips of his hoofs clawing at the ground, and his great sides matted with sweat, filled everyone with admiration. Clover warned him sometimes to be careful not to overstrain himself, but Boxer would never listen to her. His two slogans, 'I will work harder' and 'Napoleon is always right', seemed to him a sufficient answer to all problems. He had made arrange-ments with the cockerel to call him three-quarters of an hour earlier in the morning instead of half an hour. And in his spare moments, of which there were not many nowadays, he would go alone to the quarry, collect a load of broken stone, and drag it down to the site of the windmill unassisted.

The animals were not badly off throughout that summer, in spite of the hardness of their work. If they had no more food than they had had in Jones's day, at least they did not have less. The advantage of only having to feed themselves, and not having to support five extravagant human beings as well, was so great that it would have taken a lot of failures to outweigh it. And in many ways the animal method of doing things was more efficient and saved labour. Such jobs as weeding, for instance, could be done with a thoroughness impossible to human beings. And again, since no animal now stole, it was unnecessary to fence off pasture from arable land, which saved a lot of labour on the upkeep of hedges and gates. Nevertheless, as the summer wore on, various unforeseen shortages began to make themselves felt. There was need of paraffin oil, nails, string, dog biscuits, and iron for the horses' shoes, none of which could be produced on the farm. Later there would also be need for seeds and artificial manure, besides various tools and, finally, the machinery for the windmill. How these were to be procured, no one was able to imagine.

One Sunday morning, when the animals assembled to receive their orders, Napoleon announced that he had decided upon a new policy. From now onwards Animal Farm would engage in trade with the neighbouring farms: not, of course, for any commercial purpose, but simply in order to obtain certain materials which were urgently necessary. The needs of the windmill must override everything else, he said. He was therefore making arrangements to sell a stack of hay and part of the current year's wheat crop, and later on, if more money were needed, it would have to be made up by the sale of eggs, for which there was always a market in Willingdon. The hens, said Napoleon, should welcome this sacrifice as their own special contribution towards the building of the windmill.

Once again the animals were conscious of a vague uneasiness. Never to have any dealings with human beings, never to engage in trade, never to make use of money—had not these been among the earliest resolutions passed at that first triumphant Meeting after Jones was expelled? All the animals remembered passing such resolutions: or at least they thought that they remembered it. The four young pigs who had protested when Napoleon abolished the Meetings raised their voices timidly, but they were promptly silenced by a tremendous growling from the dogs. Then, as usual, the sheep broke into 'Four legs good, two legs bad!' and the momentary awkwardness was smoothed over. Finally Napoleon raised his trotter for silence and announced that he had already made all the arrangements. There would be no need for any of the animals to come in contact with human beings, which would clearly be most undesirable. He intended to take the whole burden upon his own shoulders. A Mr. Whymper, a solicitor living in Willingdon, had agreed to act as intermediary between Animal Farm and the outside world, and would visit the farm every Monday morning to receive his instructions. Napoleon ended his speech with his usual cry of 'Long live Animal Farm!', and after the singing of 'Beasts of England' the animals were dismissed.

Afterwards Squealer made a round of the farm and set the animals' minds at rest. He assured them that the resolution against engaging in trade and using money had never been passed, or even suggested. It was pure imagination, probably traceable in the beginning to lies circulated by Snowball. A few animals still felt faintly doubtful, but Squealer asked them shrewdly, 'Are you certain that this is not something that you have dreamed, comrades? Have you any record of such a resolution? Is it written down anywhere?' And since it was certainly true that nothing of the kind existed in writing, the animals were satisfied that they had been mistaken.

Every Monday Mr. Whymper visited the farm as had been arranged. He was a sly-looking little man with side whiskers, a solicitor in a very small way of business, but sharp enough to have realized earlier than anyone else that Animal Farm would need a broker and that the commissions would be worth having. The animals watched his coming and going with a kind of dread, and avoided him as much as possible. Nevertheless, the sight of Napoleon, on all fours, delivering orders to Whymper, who stood on two legs, roused their pride and partly reconciled them to the new arrangement. Their relations with the human race were now not quite the same as they had been before. The human beings did not hate Animal Farm any less now that it was prospering; indeed, they hated it more than ever. Every human being held it as an article of faith that the farm would go bankrupt sooner or later, and, above all, that the windmill would be a failure. They would meet in the public-houses and prove to one another by means of diagrams that the windmill was bound to fall down, or that if it did stand up, then that it would never work. And yet, against their will, they had developed a certain respect for the efficiency with which the animals were managing their own affairs. One symptom of this was that they had begun to call Animal Farm by its proper name and ceased to pretend that it was called the Manor Farm. They had also dropped their championship of Jones, who had given up hope of getting his farm back and gone to live in another part of the country. Except through Whymper, there was as yet no contact between Animal Farm and the outside world, but there were constant rumours that Napoleon was about to enter into a definite business agreement either with Mr. Pilkington of Foxwood or with Mr. Frederick of Pinchfield—but never, it was noticed, with both simultaneously.

It was about this time that the pigs suddenly moved into the farmhouse and took up their residence there. Again the animals seemed to remember that a resolution against this had been passed in the early days, and again Squealer was able to convince them that this was not the case. It was absolutely necessary, he said, that the pigs, who were the brains of the farm, should have a quiet place to work in. It was also more suited to the dignity of the Leader (for of late he had taken to speaking of Napoleon under the title of 'Leader') to live in a house than in a mere sty. Nevertheless, some of the animals were disturbed when they heard that the pigs not only took their meals in the kitchen and used the drawing-room as a recreation room, but also slept in the beds. Boxer passed it off as usual with 'Napoleon is always right!', but Clover, who thought she remembered a definite ruling against beds, went to the end of the barn and tried to puzzle out the Seven Commandments which were inscribed there. Finding herself unable to read more than individual letters, she fetched Muriel.

'Muriel,' she said, 'read me the Fourth Commandment. Does it not say something about never sleeping in a bed?'

With some difficulty Muriel spelt it out.

'It says, "No animal shall sleep in a bed *with sheets*",' she announced finally.

Curiously enough, Clover had not remembered that the Fourth Commandment mentioned sheets; but as it was there on the wall, it must have done so. And Squealer, who happened to be passing at this moment, attended by two or three dogs, was able to put the whole matter in its proper perspective.

'You have heard then, comrades,' he said, 'that we pigs now sleep in the beds of the farmhouse? And why not? You did not suppose surely, that there was ever a ruling against *beds*? A bed merely means a place to sleep in. A pile of straw in a stall is a bed, properly regarded. The rule was against *sheets*, which are a human invention. We have removed the sheets from the farmhouse beds, and sleep between blankets. And very comfortable beds they are too! But not more comfortable than we need, I can tell you, comrades, with all the brainwork we have to do nowadays. You would not rob us of our repose, would you, comrades? You would not have us too tired to carry out our duties? Surely none of you wishes to see Jones back?'

The animals reassured him on this point immediately, and no more was said about the pigs sleeping in the farmhouse beds. And when some days afterwards, it was announced that from now on the pigs would get up an hour later in the mornings than the other animals, no complaint was made about that either.

By the autumn the animals were tired but happy. They had had a hard year, and after the sale of part of the hay and corn, the stores of food for the winter were none too plentiful, but the windmill compensated for everything. It was almost half built now. After the harvest there was a stretch of clear dry weather, and the animals toiled harder than ever, thinking it well worth while to plod to and fro all day with blocks of stone if by doing so they could raise the walls another foot. Boxer would even come out at nights and work for an hour or two on his own by the light of the harvest moon. In their spare moments the animals would walk round and round the half-finished mill, admiring the strength and perpendicularity of its walls and marvelling that they should ever have been able to build anything so imposing. Only old Benjamin refused to grow enthusiastic about the windmill, though, as usual, he would utter nothing beyond the cryptic remark that donkeys live a long time.

November came, with raging south-west winds. Building had to stop because it was now too wet to mix the cement. Finally there came a night when the gale was so violent that the farm buildings rocked on their foundations and several tiles were blown off the roof of the barn. The hens woke up squawking with terror because they had all dreamed simultaneously of hearing a gun go off in the distance. In the morning the animals came out of their stalls to find that the flagstaff had blown down and an elm tree at the foot of the orchard had been plucked up like a radish. They had just noticed this when a cry of despair broke from every animal's throat. A terrible sight had met their eyes. The windmill was in ruins.

With one accord they dashed down to the spot. Napoleon, who seldom moved out of a walk, raced ahead of them all. Yes, there it lay, the fruit of all their struggles, levelled to its foundations, the stones they had broken and carried so laboriously scattered all around. Unable at first to speak, they stood gazing mournfully at the litter of fallen stone. Napoleon paced to and fro in silence, occasionally snuffing at the ground. His tail had grown rigid and twitched sharply from side to side, a sign in him of intense mental activity. Suddenly he halted as though his mind were made up.

'Comrades,' he said quietly, 'do you know who is responsible for this? Do you know the enemy who has come in the night and overthrown our windmill? SNOWBALL!' he suddenly roared in a voice of thunder. 'Snowball has done this thing! In sheer malignity, thinking to set back our plans and avenge himself for his ignominious expulsion, this traitor has crept here under cover of night and destroyed our work of nearly a year. Comrades, here and now I pronounce the death sentence upon Snowball. "Animal Hero, Second Class", and half a bushel of apples to any animal who brings him to justice. A full bushel to anyone who captures him alive!'

The animals were shocked beyond measure to learn that even Snowball could be guilty of such an action. There was a cry of indignation, and everyone began thinking out ways of catching Snowball if he should ever come back. Almost immediately the footprints of a pig were discovered in the grass at a little distance from the knoll. They could only be traced for a few yards, but appeared to lead to a hole in the hedge. Napoleon snuffed deeply at them and pronounced them to be Snowball's. He gave it as his opinion that Snowball had probably come from the direction of Foxwood Farm.

'No more delays, comrades!' said Napoleon when the footprints had been examined. 'There is work to be done. This very morning we will begin rebuilding the windmill, and we will build all through the winter, rain or shine. We will teach this miserable traitor that he cannot undo our work so easily. Remember, comrades, there must be no alteration in our plans: they shall be carried out to the day. Forward, comrades! Long live the windmill! Long live Animal Farm!'

CHAPTER 7

I T was a bitter winter. The stormy weather was followed by sleet and snow, and then by a hard frost which did not break till well into February. The animals carried on as best they could with the rebuilding of the windmill, well knowing that the outside world was watching them and that the envious human beings would rejoice and triumph if the mill were not finished on time.

Out of spite, the human beings pretended not to believe that it was Snowball who had destroyed the windmill: they said that it had fallen down because the walls were too thin. The animals knew that this was not the case. Still, it had been decided to build the walls three feet thick this time instead of eighteen inches as before, which meant collecting much larger quantities of stone. For a long time the quarry was full of snowdrifts and nothing could be done. Some progress was made in the dry frosty weather that followed, but it was cruel work, and the animals could not feel so hopeful about it as they had felt before. They were always cold, and usually hungry as well. Only Boxer and Clover never lost heart. Squealer made excellent speeches on the joy of service and the dignity of labour, but the other animals found more inspiration in

45

Boxer's strength and his never-failing cry of 'I will work harder!'

In January food fell short. The corn ration was drastically reduced, and it was announced that an extra potato ration would be issued to make up for it. Then it was discovered that the greater part of the potato crop had been frosted in the clamps, which had not been covered thickly enough. The potatoes had become soft and discoloured, and only a few were edible. For days at a time the animals had nothing to eat but chaff and mangels. Starvation seemed to stare them in the face.

It was vitally necessary to conceal this fact from the outside world. Emboldened by the collapse of the windmill, the human beings were inventing fresh lies about Animal Farm. Once again it was being put about that all the animals were dying of famine and disease, and that they were continually fighting among themselves and had resorted to cannibalism and infanticide. Napoleon was well aware of the bad results that might follow if the real facts of the food situation were known, and he decided to make use of Mr. Whymper to spread a contrary impression. Hitherto the animals had had little or no contact with Whymper on his weekly visits: now however, a few selected animals, mostly sheep, were instructed to remark casually in his hearing that rations had been increased. In addition, Napoleon ordered the almost empty bins in the store-shed to be filled nearly to the brim with sand, which was then covered up with what remained of the grain and meal. On some suitable pretext Whymper was led through the store-shed and allowed to catch a glimpse of the bins. He was deceived and continued to report to the outside world that there was no food shortage on Animal Farm.

Nevertheless, towards the end of January it became obvious that it would be necessary to procure some more grain from somewhere. In these days Napoleon rarely appeared in public, but spent all his time in the farmhouse, which was guarded at each door by fierce-looking dogs. When he did emerge, it was in a ceremonial manner, with an escort of six dogs who closely surrounded him and growled if anyone came too near. Frequently he did not even appear on Sunday mornings, but issued his orders through one of the other pigs, usually Squealer.

One Sunday morning Squealer announced that the hens, who had just come in to lay again, must surrender their eggs. Napoleon had accepted, through Whymper, a contract for four hundred eggs a week. The price of these would pay for enough grain and meal to keep the farm going till summer came on and conditions were easier.

When the hens heard this, they raised a terrible outcry. They had been warned earlier that this sacrifice might be necessary, but had not believed that it would really happen. They were just getting their clutches ready for the spring sitting, and they protested that to take the eggs away now was murder. For the first time since the expulsion of Jones there was something resembling a rebellion. Led by three young Black Minorca pullets, the hens made a determined effort to thwart Napoleon's wishes. Their method was to fly up to the rafters and there lay their eggs, which smashed to pieces on the floor. Napoleon acted swiftly and ruthlessly. He ordered the hens' rations to be stopped, and decreed that any animal giving so much as a grain of corn to a hen should be punished by death. The dogs saw to it that these orders were carried out. For five days the hens held out, then they capitulated and went back to their nesting boxes. Nine hens had died in the meantime. Their bodies were buried in the orchard, and it was given out that they had died of coccidiosis. Whymper heard nothing of this affair, and the eggs were duly delivered, a grocer's van driving up to the farm once a week to take them away.

All this while no more had been seen of Snowball. He was rumoured to be hiding on one of the neighbouring farms, either Foxwood or Pinchfield. Napoleon was by this time on slightly better terms with the other farmers than before. It happened that there was in the yard a pile of timber which had been stacked there ten years earlier when a beech spinney was cleared. It was well seasoned, and Whymper had advised Napoleon to sell it; both Mr. Pilkington and Mr. Frederick were anxious to buy it. Napoleon was hesitating between the two, unable to make up his mind. It was noticed that whenever he seemed on the point of coming to an agreement with Frederick, Snowball was declared to be hiding at Foxwood, while, when he inclined towards Pilkington, Snowball was said to be at Pinchfield.

Suddenly, early in the spring, an alarming thing was discovered. Snowball was secretly frequenting the farm by night! The animals were so disturbed that they could hardly sleep in their stalls. Every night, it was said, he came creeping in under cover of darkness and performed all kinds of mischief. He stole the corn, he upset the milk-pails, he broke the eggs, he trampled the seed-beds, he gnawed the bark off the fruit trees. Whenever anything went wrong it became usual to attribute it to Snowball. If a window was broken or a drain blocked up, someone was certain to say that Snowball had come in the night and done it, and when the key of the store-shed was lost, the whole farm was convinced that Snowball had thrown it down the well. Curiously enough, they went on believing this even after the mislaid key was found under a sack of meal. The cows declared unanimously that Snowball crept into their stalls and milked them in their sleep. The rats, which had been troublesome that winter, were also said to be in league with Snowball.

Napoleon decreed that there should be a full investigation into Snowball's activities. With his dogs in attendance he set out and made a careful tour of inspection of the farm buildings, the other animals following at a respectful distance. At every few steps Napoleon stopped and snuffed the ground for traces of Snowball's footsteps, which, he said, he could detect by the smell. He snuffed in every corner, in the barn, in the cowshed, in the hen-houses, in the vegetable garden, and found traces of Snowball almost everywhere. He would put his snout to the ground, give several deep sniffs, and exclaim in a terrible voice, 'Snowball! He has been here! I can smell him distinctly!' and at the word 'Snowball' all the dogs let out blood-curdling growls and showed their side teeth.

The animals were thoroughly frightened. It seemed to them as though Snowball were some kind of invisible influence, pervading the air about them and menacing them with all kinds of dangers. In the evening Squealer called them together, and with an alarmed expression on his face told them that he had some serious news to report.

'Comrades!' cried Squealer, making little nervous skips, 'a most terrible thing has been discovered. Snowball has sold himself to Frederick of Pinchfield Farm, who is even now plotting to attack us and take our farm away from us! Snowball is to act as his guide when the attack begins. But there is worse than that. We had thought that Snowball's rebellion was caused by his vanity and ambition. But we were wrong, comrades. Do you know what the real reason was? Snowball was in league with Jones from the very start! He was Jones's secret agent all the time. It has all been proved by documents which he left behind him and which we have only just discovered. To my mind this explains a great deal, comrades. Did we not see for ourselves how he attempted—fortunately without success—to get us defeated and destroyed at the Battle of the Cowshed?'

The animals were stupefied. This was a wickedness far outdoing Snowball's destruction of the windmill. But it was some minutes before they could fully take it in. They all remembered, or thought they remembered, how they had seen Snowball charging ahead of them at the Battle of the Cowshed, how he had rallied and encouraged them at every turn, and how he had not paused for an instant even when the pellets from Jones's gun had wounded his back. At first it was a little difficult to see how this fitted in with his being on Jones's side. Even Boxer, who seldom asked questions, was puzzled. He lay down, tucked his fore-hoofs beneath him, shut his eyes, and with a hard effort managed to formulate his thoughts.

'I do not believe that,' he said. 'Snowball fought bravely at the Battle of the Cowshed. I saw him myself. Did we not give him "Animal Hero, First Class", immediately afterwards?'

'That was our mistake, comrade. For we know now—it is all written down in the secret documents that we have found—that in reality he was trying to lure us to our doom.'

'But he was wounded,' said Boxer. 'We all saw him running with blood.'

'That was part of the arrangement!' cried Squealer. 'Jones's shot only grazed him. I could show you this in his own writing, if you were able to read it. The plot was for Snowball, at the critical moment, to give the signal for flight and leave the field to the enemy. And he very nearly succeeded—I will even say, comrades, he *would* have succeeded if it had not been for our heroic Leader, Comrade Napoleon. Do you not remember how, just at the moment when Jones and his men had got inside the yard, Snowball suddenly turned and fled, and many animals followed him? And do you not remember, too, that it was just at that moment, when panic was spreading and all seemed lost, that Comrade Napoleon sprang forward with a cry of "Death to Humanity!" and sank his teeth in Jones's leg? Surely you remember *that*, comrades?' exclaimed Squealer frisking from side to side.

Now when Squealer described the scene so graphically, it seemed to the animals that they did remember it. At any rate, they remembered that at the critical moment of the battle Snowball had turned to flee. But Boxer was still a little uneasy.

'I do not believe that Snowball was a traitor at the beginning,' he said finally. 'What he has done since is different. But

I believe that at the Battle of the Cowshed he was a good comrade.'

'Our Leader, Comrade Napoleon,' announced Squealer, speaking very slowly and firmly, 'has stated categorically—categorically, comrade—that Snowball was Jones's agent from the very beginning—yes, and from long before the Rebellion was ever thought of.'

'Ah, that is different!' said Boxer. 'If Comrade Napoleon says it, it must be right.'

'That is the true spirit, comrade!' cried Squealer, but it was noticed he cast a very ugly look at Boxer with his little twinkling eyes. He turned to go, then paused and added impressively: 'I warn every animal on this farm to keep his eyes very wide open. For we have reason to think that some of Snowball's secret agents are lurking among us at this moment!'

Four days later, in the late afternoon, Napoleon ordered all the animals to assemble in the yard. When they were all gathered together, Napoleon emerged from the farmhouse, wearing both his medals (for he had recently awarded himself 'Animal Hero, First Class', and 'Animal Hero, Second Class'), with his nine huge dogs frisking round him and uttering growls that sent shivers down all the animals' spines. They all cowered silently in their places, seeming to know in advance that some terrible thing was about to happen.

Napoleon stood sternly surveying his audience; then he uttered a high-pitched whimper. Immediately the dogs bounded forward, seized four of the pigs by the ear and dragged them, squealing with pain and terror, to Napoleon's feet. The pigs' ears were bleeding, the dogs had tasted blood, and for a few moments they appeared to go quite mad. To the amazement of everybody, three of them flung themselves upon Boxer. Boxer saw them coming and put out his great hoof, caught a dog in mid-air, and pinned him to the ground. The dog shrieked for mercy and the other two fled with their tails between their legs. Boxer looked at Napoleon to know whether he should crush the dog to death or let it go. Napoleon appeared to change countenance, and sharply ordered Boxer to let the dog go, whereat Boxer lifted his hoof, and the dog slunk away, bruised and howling.

Presently the tumult died down. The four pigs waited, trembling, with guilt written on every line of their countenances. Napoleon now called upon them to confess their crimes. They were the same four pigs as had protested when Napoleon abolished the Sunday Meetings. Without any further prompting they confessed that they had been secretly in touch with Snowball ever since his expulsion, that they had collaborated with him in destroying the windmill, and that they had entered into an agreement with him to hand over Animal Farm to Mr. Frederick. They added that Snowball had privately admitted to them that he had been Jones's secret agent for years past. When they had finished their confession, the dogs promptly tore their throats out, and in a terrible voice Napoleon demanded whether any other animal had anything to confess.

The three hens who had been the ringleaders in the attempted rebellion over the eggs now came forward and stated that Snowball had appeared to them in a dream and incited them to disobey Napoleon's orders. They, too, were slaughtered. Then a goose came forward and confessed to having secreted six ears of corn during the last year's harvest and eaten them in the night. Then a sheep confessed to having urinated in the drinking pool—urged to do this, so she said, by Snowball—and two other sheep confessed to having murdered an old ram, an especially devoted follower of Napoleon, by chasing him round and round a bonfire when he was suffering from a cough. They were all slain on the spot. And so the tale of confessions and executions went on, until there was a pile of corpses lying before Napoleon's feet and the air was heavy with the smell of blood, which had been unknown there since the expulsion of Jones.

When it was all over, the remaining animals, except for the pigs and dogs, crept away in a body. They were shaken and miserable. They did not know which was more shocking—the treachery of the animals who had leagued themselves with Snowball, or the cruel retribution they had just witnessed. In the old days there had often been scenes of bloodshed equally terrible, but it seemed to all of them that it was far worse now that it was happening among themselves. Since Jones had left the farm, until today, no animal had killed another animal. Not even a rat had been killed. They had made their way on to the little knoll where the half-finished windmill stood, and with one accord they all lay down as though huddling together for warmth—Clover, Muriel, Benjamin, the cows, the sheep, and a whole flock of geese and hens—everyone, indeed, except the cat, who had suddenly disappeared just before Napoleon ordered the animals to assemble. For some time nobody spoke. Only Boxer remained on his feet. He fidgeted to and fro, swishing his long black tail against his sides, and occassionally uttering a little whinny of surprise. Finally he said:

'I do not understand it. I would not have believed that such things could happen on our farm. It must be due to some fault in ourselves. The solution, as I see it, is to work harder. From now onwards I shall get up a full hour earlier in the mornings.'

And he moved off at his lumbering trot and made for the quarry. Having got there, he collected two successive loads of stone and dragged them down to the windmill before retiring for the night.

The animals huddled about Clover, not speaking. The knoll where they were lying gave them a wide prospect across the countryside. Most of Animal Farm was within their view— the long pasture stretching down to the main road, the hay-field, the spinney, the drinking pool, the ploughed fields where the young wheat was thick and green, and the red roofs of the farm buildings with the smoke curling from the chimneys. It was a clear spring evening. The grass and the bursting hedges were gilded by the level rays of the sun. Never had the farm—and with a kind of surprise they remembered that it was their own farm, every inch of it their own property—appeared to the animals so desirable a place. As Clover looked down the hillside her eyes filled with tears. If she could have spoken her thoughts, it would have been to say that this was not what they had aimed at when they had set themselves years ago to work for the overthrow of the human race. These scenes of terror and slaughter were not what they had looked forward to on that night when old Major first stirred them to rebellion. If she herself had had any picture of the future, it had been of a society of animals set free from hunger and the whip, all equal, each working according to his capacity, the strong protecting the weak, as she had protected the last brood of ducklings with her foreleg on the night of Major's speech. Instead—she did not know why —they had come to a time when no one dared speak his mind, when fierce, growling dogs roamed everywhere, and when you had to watch your comrades torn to pieces after confessing to shocking crimes. There was no thought of rebellion or disobedience in her mind. She knew that, even as things were, they were far better off than they had been in the days of Jones, and that before all else it was needful to prevent the return of the human beings. Whatever happened she would remain faithful, work hard, carry out the orders that were given to her, and accept the leadership of Napoleon. But still, it was not for this that she and all the other animals had hoped and toiled. It was not for this that they had built the windmill and faced the bullets of Jones's guns. Such were her thoughts, though she lacked the words to express them.

At last, feeling this to be in some way a substitute for the words she was unable to find, she began to sing 'Beasts of England'. The other animals sitting round her took it up, and

54

they sang it three times over—very tunefully, but slowly and mournfully, in a way they had never sung it before.

They had just finished singing it for the third time when Squealer, attended by two dogs, approached them with the air of having something important to say. He announced that, by a special decree of Comrade Napoleon. 'Beasts of England' had been abolished. From now onwards it was forbidden to sing it.

The animals were taken aback.

'Why?' cried Muriel.

'It is no longer needed, comrade,' said Squealer stiffly. '"Beasts of England" was the song of the Rebellion. But the Rebellion is now completed. The execution of the traitors this afternoon was the final act. The enemy both external and internal has been defeated. In "Beasts of England" we expressed our longing for a better society in days to come. But that society has now been established. Clearly this song has no longer any purpose.'

Frightened though they were, some of the animals might possibly have protested, but at this moment the sheep set up their usual bleating of 'Four legs good, two legs bad', which went on for several minutes and put an end to the discussion.

So 'Beasts of England' was heard no more. In its place Minimus, the poet, had composed another song which began:

Animal Farm, Animal Farm,
Never through me shalt thou come to harm!

and this was sung every Sunday morning after the hoisting of the flag. But somehow neither the words nor the tune ever seemed to the animals to come up to 'Beasts of England'.

CHAPTER 8

A FEW days later, when the terror caused by the executions had died down, some of the animals remembered—or thought they remembered—that the Sixth Commandment decreed: 'No animal shall kill any other animal.' And though no one cared to mention it in the hearing of the pigs or the dogs, it was felt that the killings which had taken place did not square with this. Clover asked Benjamin to read her the Sixth Commandment, and when Benjamin, as usual, said that he refused to meddle in such matters, she fetched Muriel. Muriel read the Commandment for her. It ran: 'No animal shall kill any other animal *without cause*.' Somehow or other, the last two words had slipped out of the animals' memory. But they saw now that the commandment had not been violated; for clearly there was good reason for killing the traitors who had leagued themselves with Snowball.

Throughout that year the animals worked even harder than they had worked in the previous year. To rebuild the windmill, with walls twice as thick as before, and to finish it by the appointed date, together with the regular work of the farm, was a tremendous labour. There were times when it seemed to the animals that they worked longer hours and fed no better than they had done in Jones's day. On Sunday mornings Squealer, holding down a long strip of paper with his trotter, would read out to them lists of figures proving that the production of every class of foodstuff had increased by 200 per cent, 300 per cent, or 500 per cent, as the case might be. The animals saw no reason to disbelieve him, especially as they could no longer remember very clearly what conditions had been like before the Rebellion. All the same, there were days when they felt that they would sooner have had less figures and more food.

All orders were now issued through Squealer or one of the other pigs. Napoleon himself was not seen in public as often as once a fortnight. When he did appear, he was attended not only by his retinue of dogs but by a black cockerel who marched in front of him and acted as a kind of trumpeter, letting out a loud 'cock-a-doodle-doo' before Napoleon spoke. Even in the farmhouse, it was said, Napoleon inhabited separate apartments from the others. He took his meals alone, with two dogs to wait upon him, and always ate from the Crown Derby dinner service which had been in the glass cupboard in the drawing-room. It was also announced that the gun would be fired every year on Napoleon's birthday, as well as on the other two anniversaries.

Napoleon was now never spoken of simply as 'Napoleon'. He was always referred to in formal style as 'our Leader, Comrade Napoleon', and the pigs liked to invent for him such titles as Father of All Animals, Terror of Mankind, Protector of the Sheep-Fold, Ducklings' Friend, and the like. In his speeches, Squealer would talk with the tears rolling down his cheeks of Napoleon's wisdom, the goodness of his heart, and the deep love he bore to all animals everywhere, even and especially the unhappy animals who still lived in ignorance and slavery on other farms. It had become usual to give Napoleon the credit for every successful achievement and every stroke of good fortune. You would often hear one hen remark to another, 'Under the guidance of our Leader, Comrade Napoleon, I have laid five eggs in six days'; or two cows, enjoying a drink at the pool, would exclaim, 'Thanks to the leadership of Comrade Napoleon, how excellent this water tastes!' The general feeling on the farm was well expressed in a poem entitled 'Comrade Napoleon', which was composed by Minimus and which ran as follows:

> *Friend of the fatherless!*
> *Fountain of happiness!*

Lord of the swill-bucket! Oh, how my soul is on
Fire when I gaze at thy
Calm and commanding eye,
Like the sun in the sky,
Comrade Napoleon!

Thou art the giver of
All that thy creatures love,
Full belly twice a day, clean straw to roll upon;
Every beast great or small
Sleeps at peace in his stall,
Thou watchest over all,
Comrade Napoleon!

Had I a sucking-pig,
Ere he had grown as big
Even as a pint bottle or a rolling-pin,
He should have learned to be
Faithful and true to thee,
Yes, his first squeak should be
'Comrade Napoleon!'

Napoleon approved of this poem and caused it to be inscribed on the wall of the big barn, at the opposite end from the Seven Commandments. It was surmounted by a portrait of Napoleon, in profile, executed by Squealer in white paint.

Meanwhile, through the agency of Whymper, Napoleon was engaged in complicated negotiations with Frederick and Pilkington. The pile of timber was still unsold. Of the two, Frederick was the more anxious to get hold of it, but he would not offer a reasonable price. At the same time there were renewed rumours that Frederick and his men were plotting to attack Animal Farm and to destroy the windmill, the building of which had aroused furious jealousy in him. Snowball was known to be still skulking on Pinchfield Farm. In the middle of the summer the animals were alarmed to hear that three hens had come forward and confessed that, inspired by Snowball, they had entered into a plot to murder Napoleon. They were executed immediately, and fresh precautions for Napoleon's safety were taken. Four dogs guarded his bed at night, one at each corner, and a young pig named Pinkeye was given the task of tasting all his food before he ate it, lest it should be poisoned.

At about the same time it was given out that Napoleon had arranged to sell the pile of timber to Mr. Pilkington; he was also going to enter into a regular agreement for the exchange of certain products between Animal Farm and Foxwood. The relations between Napoleon and Pilkington, though they were only conducted through Whymper, were now almost friendly. The animals distrusted Pilkington, as a human being, but greatly preferred him to Frederick, whom they both feared and hated. As the summer wore on, and the windmill neared completion, the rumours of an impending treacherous attack grew stronger and stronger. Frederick, it was said, intended to bring against them twenty men all armed with guns, and he had already bribed the magistrates and police, so that if he could once get hold of the title-deeds of Animal Farm they would ask no questions. Moreover, terrible stories were leaking out from Pinchfield about the cruelties that Frederick practised upon his animals. He had flogged an old horse to death, he starved his cows, he had killed a dog by throwing it into a furnace, he amused himself in the evenings by making cocks fight with splinters of razor-blade tied to their spurs. The animals' blood boiled with rage when they heard of these things being done to their comrades, and sometimes they clamoured to be allowed to go out in a body and attack Pinchfield Farm, drive out the humans, and set the animals free. But Squealer counselled them to avoid rash actions and trust in Comrade Napoleon's strategy.

Nevertheless, feeling against Frederick continued to run

high. One Sunday morning Napoleon appeared in the barn and explained that he had never at any time contemplated selling the pile of timber to Frederick; he considered it beneath his dignity, he said, to have dealings with scoundrels of that description. The pigeons who were still sent out to spread tidings of the Rebellion were forbidden to set foot anywhere on Foxwood, and were also ordered to drop their former slogan of 'Death to Humanity' in favour of 'Death to Frederick'. In the late summer yet another of Snowball's machinations was laid bare. The wheat crop was full of weeds, and it was discovered that on one of his nocturnal visits Snowball had mixed weed seeds with the seed corn. A gander who had been privy to the plot had confessed his guilt to Squealer and immediately committed suicide by swallowing deadly night-shade berries. The animals now also learned that Snowball had never—as many of them had believed hitherto—received the order of 'Animal Hero, First Class'. This was merely a legend which had been spread some time after the Battle of the Cow-shed by Snowball himself. So far from being decorated, he had been censured for showing cowardice in the battle. Once again some of the animals heard this with a certain bewilderment, but Squealer was soon able to convince them that their memories had been at fault.

In the autumn, by a tremendous, exhausting effort—for the harvest had to be gathered at almost the same time—the windmill was finished. The machinery had still to be installed, and Whymper was negotiating the purchase of it, but the structure was completed. In the teeth of every difficulty, in spite of inexperience, of primitive implements, of bad luck, and of Snowball's treachery, the work had been finished punctually to the very day! Tired out but proud, the animals walked round and round their masterpiece, which appeared even more beautiful in their eyes than when it had been built the first time. Moreover, the walls were twice as thick as before. Nothing short of explosives would lay them low this time! And when they thought of how they had laboured, what discouragements they had overcome, and the enormous difference that would be made in their lives when the sails were turning and the dynamos running—when they thought of all this, their tiredness forsook them and they gambolled round and round the windmill, uttering cries of triumph. Napoleon himself, attended by his dogs and his cockerel, came down to inspect the completed work; he personally congratulated the animals on their achievement, and announced that the mill would be named Napoleon Mill.

Two days later the animals were called together for a special meeting in the barn. They were struck dumb with surprise when Napoleon announced that he had sold the pile of timber to Frederick. Tomorrow Frederick's wagons would arrive and begin carting it away. Throughout the whole period of his seeming friendship with Pilkington, Napoleon had really been in secret agreement with Frederick.

All relations with Foxwood had been broken off; insulting messages had been sent to Pilkington. The pigeons had been told to avoid Pinchfield Farm and to alter their slogan from 'Death to Frederick' to 'Death to Pilkington'. At the same time Napoleon assured the animals that the stories of an impending attack on Animal Farm were completely untrue, and that the tales about Frederick's cruelty to his animals had been greatly exaggerated. All these rumours had probably originated with Snowball and his agents. It now appeared that Snowball was not, after all, hiding on Pinchfield Farm, and in fact had never been there in his life: he was living—in considerable luxury, so it was said—at Foxwood, and had in reality been a pensioner of Pilkington for years past.

The pigs were in ecstasies over Napoleon's cunning. By seeming to be friendly with Pilkington he had forced Frederick to raise his price by twelve pounds. But the superior quality of Napoleon's mind, said Squealer, was shown in the fact that he trusted nobody, not even Frederick. Frederick had wanted to pay for the timber with something called a cheque, which, it seemed, was a piece of paper with a promise to pay written upon it. But Napoleon was too clever for him. He had demanded payment in real five-pound notes, which were to be handed over before the timber was removed. Already Frederick had paid up; and the sum he had paid was just enough to buy the machinery for the windmill.

Meanwhile the timber was being carted away at high speed. When it was all gone, another special meeting was held in the barn for the animals to inspect Frederick's banknotes. Smiling beatifically, and wearing both his decorations, Napoleon reposed on a bed of straw on the platform, with the money at his side, neatly piled on a china dish from the farmhouse kitchen. The animals filed slowly past, and each gazed his fill. And Boxer put out his nose to sniff at the banknotes, and the flimsy white things stirred and rustled in his breath.

Three days later there was a terrible hullabaloo. Whymper, his face deadly pale, came racing up the path on his bicycle, flung it down in the yard, and rushed straight into the farmhouse. The next moment a choking roar of rage sounded from Napoleon's apartments. The news of what had happened sped round the farm like wildfire. The bank-notes were forgeries! Frederick had got the timber for nothing!

Napoleon called the animals together immediately and in a terrible voice pronounced the death sentence upon Frederick. When captured, he said, Frederick should be boiled alive. At the same time he warned them that after this treacherous deed the worst was to be expected. Frederick and his men might make their long-expected attack at any moment. Sentinels were placed at all the approaches to the farm. In addition, four pigeons were sent to Foxwood with a conciliatory message, which it was hoped might re-establish good relations with Pilkington.

The very next morning the attack came. The animals were

at breakfast when the look-outs came racing in with the news that Frederick and his followers had already come through the five-barred gate. Boldly enough the animals sallied forth to meet them, but this time they did not have the easy victory that they had had in the Battle of the Cowshed. There were fifteen men, with half a dozen guns between them, and they opened fire as soon as they got within fifty yards. The animals could not face the terrible explosions and the stinging pellets, and in spite of the efforts of Napoleon and Boxer to rally them, they were soon driven back. A number of them were already wounded. They took refuge in the farm buildings and peeped cautiously out from chinks and knot-holes. The whole of the big pasture, including the windmill, was in the hands of the enemy. For the moment even Napoleon seemed at a loss. He paced up and down without a word, his tail rigid and twitching. Wistful glances were sent in the direction of Foxwood. If Pilkington and his men would help them, the day might yet be won. But at the moment the four pigeons, who had been sent out on the day before, returned, one of them bearing a scrap of paper from Pilkington. On it was pencilled the words: 'Serves you right'.

Meanwhile Frederick and his men had halted about the windmill. The animals watched them, and a murmur of dismay went round. Two of the men had produced a crowbar and a sledge hammer. They were going to knock the windmill down.

'Impossible!' cried Napoleon. 'We have built the walls far too thick for that. They could not knock it down in a week. Courage, comrades!'

But Benjamin was watching the movements of the men intently. The two with the hammer and the crowbar were drilling a hole near the base of the windmill. Slowly, and with an air almost of amusement, Benjamin nodded his long muzzle.

'I thought so,' he said. 'Do you not see what they are doing?

In another moment they are going to pack blasting powder into that hole "

Terrified, the animals waited. It was impossible now to venture out of the shelter of the buildings. After a few minutes the men were seen to be running in all directions. Then there was a deafening roar. The pigeons swirled into the air, and all the animals, except Napoleon, flung themselves flat on their bellies and hid their faces. When they got up again, a huge cloud of black smoke was hanging where the windmill had been. Slowly the breeze drifted it away. The windmill had ceased to exist!

At this sight the animals' courage returned to them. The fear and despair they had felt a moment earlier were drowned in their rage against this vile, contemptible act. A mighty cry for vengeance went up, and without waiting for further orders they charged forth in a body and made straight for the enemy. This time they did not heed the cruel pellets that swept over them like hail. It was a savage, bitter battle. The men fired again and again, and when the animals got to close quarters, lashed out with their sticks and their heavy boots. A cow, three sheep, and two geese were killed, and nearly everyone was wounded. Even Napoleon, who was directing operations from the rear, had the tip of his tail chipped by a pellet. But the men did not go unscathed either. Three of them had their heads broken by blows from Boxer's hoofs; another was gored in the belly by a cow's horn; another had his trousers nearly torn off by Jessie and Bluebell. And when the nine dogs of Napoleon's own bodyguard, whom he had instructed to make a detour under cover of the hedge, suddenly appeared on the men's flank, baying ferociously, panic overtook them. They saw that they were in danger of being surrounded. Frederick shouted to his men to get out while the going was good, and the next moment the cowardly enemy was running for dear life. The animals chased them right down to the bottom of the field, and got in some last kicks

64

at them as they forced their way through the thorn hedge.

They had won, but they were weary and bleeding. Slowly they began to limp back towards the farm. The sight of their dead comrades stretched upon the grass moved some of them to tears. And for a little while they halted in sorrowful silence at the place where the windmill had once stood. Yes, it was gone; almost the last trace of their labour was gone! Even the foundations were partially destroyed. And in rebuilding it they could not this time, as before, make use of the fallen stones. This time the stones had vanished too. The force of the explosion had flung them to distances of hundreds of yards. It was as though the windmill had never been.

As they approached the farm Squealer, who had unaccountably been absent during the fighting, came skipping towards them, whisking his tail and beaming with satisfaction. And the animals heard, from the direction of the farm buildings, the solemn booming of a gun.

'What is that gun firing for?' said Boxer.

'To celebrate our victory!' cried Squealer.

'What victory?' said Boxer. His knees were bleeding, he had lost a shoe and split his hoof, and a dozen pellets had lodged themselves in his hindleg.

'What victory, comrade? Have we not driven the enemy off our soil—the sacred soil of Animal Farm?'

'But they have destroyed the windmill. And we had worked on it for two years!'

'What matter? We will build another windmill. We will build six windmills if we feel like it. You do not appreciate, comrade, the mighty thing that we have done. The enemy was in occupation of this very ground that we stand upon. And now—thanks to the leadership of Comrade Napoleon—we have won every inch of it back again!'

'Then we have won back what we had before,' said Boxer.

'That is our victory,' said Squealer.

They limped into the yard. The pellets under the skin of

Boxer's leg smarted painfully. He saw ahead of him the heavy labour of rebuilding the windmill from the foundations, and already in imagination he braced himself for the task. But for the first time it occurred to him that he was eleven years old and that perhaps his great muscles were not quite what they had once been.

But when the animals saw the green flag flying, and heard the gun firing again—seven times it was fired in all—and heard the speech that Napoleon made, congratulating them on their conduct, it did seem to them after all that they had won a great victory. The animals slain in the battle were given a solemn funeral. Boxer and Clover pulled the wagon which served as a hearse, and Napoleon himself walked at the head of the procession. Two whole days were given over to celebrations. There were songs, speeches, and more firing of the gun, and a special gift of an apple was bestowed on every animal, with two ounces of corn for each bird and three biscuits for each dog. It was announced that the battle would be called the Battle of the Windmill, and that Napoleon had created a new decoration, the Order of the Green Banner, which he had conferred upon himself. In the general rejoicings the unfortunate affair of the bank-notes was forgotten.

It was a few days later than this that the pigs came upon a case of whisky in the cellars of the farmhouse. It had been overlooked at the time when the house was first occupied. That night there came from the farmhouse the sound of loud singing, in which, to everyone's surprise, the strains of 'Beasts of England' were mixed up. At about half past nine Napoleon, wearing an old bowler hat of Mr. Jones's, was distinctly seen to emerge from the back door, gallop rapidly round the yard, and disappear indoors again. But in the morning a deep silence hung over the farmhouse. Not a pig appeared to be stirring. It was nearly nine o'clock when Squealer made his appearance, walking slowly and dejectedly, his eyes dull, his tail hanging limply behind him, and with every appearance of being seriously ill. He called the animals together and told them that he had a terrible piece of news to impart. Comrade Napoleon was dying!

A cry of lamentation went up. Straw was laid down outside the doors of the farmhouse, and the animals walked on tiptoe. With tears in their eyes they asked one another what they should do if their Leader were taken away from them. A rumour went round that Snowball had after all contrived to introduce poison into Napoleon's food. At eleven o'clock Squealer came out to make another announcement. As his last act upon earth, Comrade Napoleon had pronounced a solemn decree: the drinking of alcohol was to be punished by death.

By the evening, however, Napoleon appeared to be somewhat better, and the following morning Squealer was able to tell them that he was well on the way to recovery. By the evening of that day Napoleon was back at work, and on the next day it was learned that he had instructed Whymper to purchase in Willingdon some booklets on brewing and distilling. A week later Napoleon gave orders that the small paddock beyond the orchard, which it had previously been intended to set aside as a grazing-ground for animals who were past work, was to be ploughed up. It was given out that the pasture was exhausted and needed re-seeding; but it soon became known that Napoleon intended to sow it with barley.

About this time there occurred a strange incident which hardly anyone was able to understand. One night at about twelve o'clock there was a loud crash in the yard, and the animals rushed out of their stalls. It was a moonlight night. At the foot of the end wall of the big barn, where the Seven Commandments were written, there lay a ladder broken in two pieces. Squealer, temporarily stunned, was sprawling beside it, and near at hand there lay a lantern, a paint-brush, and an overturned pot of white paint. The dogs immediately made a ring round Squealer, and escorted him back to the farmhouse as soon as he was able to walk. None of the animals could form any idea as to what this meant, except old Benjamin, who nodded his muzzle with a knowing air, and seemed to understand, but would say nothing.

But a few days later Muriel, reading over the Seven Commandments to herself, noticed that there was yet another of them which the animals had remembered wrong. They had thought that the Fifth Commandment was 'No animal shall drink alcohol', but there were two words that they had forgotten. Actually the Commandment read: 'No animal shall drink alcohol *to excess*.'

CHAPTER 9

BOXER'S split hoof was a long time in healing. They had started the rebuilding of the windmill the day after the victory celebrations were ended. Boxer refused to take even a day off work, and made it a point of honour not to let it be seen that he was in pain. In the evening he would admit privately to Clover that the hoof troubled him a great deal. Clover treated the hoof with poultices of herbs which she prepared by chewing them, and both she and Benjamin urged Boxer to work less hard. 'A horse's lungs do not last for ever,' she said to him. But Boxer would not listen. He had, he said, only one real ambition left—to see the windmill well under way before he reached the age for retirement.

At the beginning, when the laws of Animal Farm were first formulated, the retiring age had been fixed for horses and pigs at twelve, for cows at fourteen, for dogs at nine, for sheep at seven, and for hens and geese at five. Liberal old age pensions had been agreed upon. As yet no animal had actually retired on pension, but of late the subject had been discussed more and more. Now that the small field beyond the orchard had been set aside for barley, it was rumoured that a corner of the large pasture was to be fenced off and turned into a grazing-ground for superannuated animals. For a horse, it was said, the pension would be five pounds of corn a day and, in winter, fifteen pounds of hay, with a carrot or possibly an apple on public holidays. Boxer's twelfth birthday was due in the late summer of the following year.

Meanwhile life was hard. The winter was as cold as the last one had been, and food was even shorter. Once again all rations were reduced, except those of the pigs and dogs. A too rigid equality in rations, Squealer explained, would have been contrary to the principles of Animalism. In any case he had no difficulty in proving to the other animals that they were *not* in reality short of food, whatever the appearances might be. For the time being, certainly, it had been found necessary to make a readjustment of rations (Squealer always spoke of it as a 'readjustment', never as a 'reduction'), but in comparison with the days of Jones, the improvement was enormous. Reading out the figures in a shrill, rapid voice, he proved to them in detail that they had more oats, more hay, more turnips than they had had in Jones's day, that they worked shorter hours, that their drinking water was of better quality, that they lived longer, that a larger proportion of their young ones survived infancy, and that they had more straw in their stalls and suffered less from fleas. The animals believed every word of it. Truth to tell, Jones and all he stood for had almost faded out of their memories. They knew that life nowadays was harsh and bare, that they were often hungry and often cold, and that they were usually working when they were not asleep. But doubtless it had been worse in the old days. They were glad to believe so. Besides, in those days they had been slaves and now they were free, and that made all the difference, as Squealer did not fail to point out.

There were many more mouths to feed now. In the autumn

the four sows had all littered about simultaneously, producing thirty-one young pigs between them. The young pigs were piebald, and as Napoleon was the only boar on the farm, it was possible to guess at their parentage. It was announced that later, when bricks and timber had been purchased, a schoolroom would be built in the farmhouse garden. For the time being, the young pigs were given their instruction by Napoleon himself in the farmhouse kitchen. They took their exercise in the garden, and were discouraged from playing with the other young animals. About this time, too, it was laid down as a rule that when a pig and any other animal met on the path, the other animal must stand aside: and also that all pigs, of whatever degree, were to have the privilege of wearing green ribbons on their tails on Sundays.

The farm had had a fairly successful year, but was still short of money. There were the bricks, sand, and lime for the schoolroom to be purchased, and it would also be necessary to begin saving up again for the machinery for the windmill. Then there were lamp oil and candles for the house, sugar for Napoleon's own table (he forbade this to the other pigs, on the ground that it made them fat), and all the usual replacements such as tools, nails, string, coal, wire, scrap-iron, and dog biscuits. A stump of hay and part of the potato crop were sold off, and the contract for eggs was increased to six hundred a week, so that that year the hens barely hatched enough chicks to keep their numbers at the same level. Rations, reduced in December, were reduced again in February, and lanterns in the stalls were forbidden, to save oil. But the pigs seemed comfortable enough, and in fact were putting on weight if anything. One afternoon in late February, a warm, rich, appetizing scent, such as the animals had never smelt before, wafted itself across the yard from the little brewhouse, which had been disused in Jones's time, and which stood beyond the kitchen. Someone said it was the smell of cooking barley. The animals sniffed the air hungrily and wondered whether a warm mash was being prepared for their supper. But no warm mash appeared, and on the following Sunday it was announced that from now onwards all barley would be reserved for the pigs. The field beyond the orchard had already been sown with barley. And the news soon leaked out that every pig was now receiving a ration of a pint of beer daily, with half a gallon for Napoleon himself, which was always served to him in the Crown Derby soup tureen.

But if there were hardships to be borne, they were partly offset by the fact that life nowadays had a greater dignity than it had had before. There were more songs, more speeches, more processions. Napoleon had commanded that once a week there should be held something called a Spontaneous Demonstration, the object of which was to celebrate the struggles and triumphs of Animal Farm. At the appointed time the animals would leave their work and march round the precincts of the farm in military formation, with the pigs leading, then the horses, then the cows, then the sheep, and then the poultry. The dogs flanked the procession and at the head of all marched Napoleon's black cockerel. Boxer and Clover always carried between them a green banner marked with the hoof and horn and the caption, 'Long live Comrade Napoleon!' Afterwards there were recitations of poems composed in Napoleon's honour, and a speech by Squealer giving particulars of the latest increases in the production of foodstuffs, and on occasion a shot was fired from the gun. The sheep were the greatest devotees of the Spontaneous Demonstration, and if anyone complained (as a few animals sometimes did, when no pigs or dogs were near) that they wasted time and meant a lot of standing about in the cold, the sheep were sure to silence him with a tremendous bleating of 'Four legs good, two legs bad!' But by and large the animals enjoyed these celebrations. They found it comforting to be reminded that, after all, they were truly their own masters and that the work they did was for their own benefit. So that, what with the songs, the processions, Squealer's lists of figures, the thunder of the gun, the crowing of the cockerel, and the fluttering of the flag, they were able to forget that their bellies were empty, at least part of the time.

In April, Animal Farm was proclaimed a Republic, and it became necessary to elect a President. There was only one candidate, Napoleon, who was elected unanimously. On the same day it was given out that fresh documents had been discovered which revealed further details about Snowball's complicity with Jones. It now appeared that Snowball had not, as the animals had previously imagined, merely attempted to lose the Battle of the Cowshed by means of a stratagem, but had been openly fighting on Jones's side. In fact, it was he who had actually been the leader of the human forces, and had charged into battle with the words 'Long live Humanity!' on his lips. The wounds on Snowball's back, which a few of the animals still remembered to have seen, had been inflicted by Napoleon's teeth.

In the middle of the summer Moses the raven suddenly reappeared on the farm, after an absence of several years. He was quite unchanged, still did not work, and talked in the same strain as ever about Sugarcandy Mountain. He would perch on a stump, flap his black wings, and talk by the hour to anyone who would listen. 'Up there, comrades,' he would say solemnly, pointing to the sky with his large beak— 'up there, just on the other side of that dark cloud that you can see—there lies Sugarcandy Mountain, that happy country where we poor animals shall rest for ever from our labours!' He even claimed to have been there on one of his higher flights, and to have seen the everlasting fields of clover and the linseed cake and lump sugar growing on the hedges. Many of the animals believed him. Their lives now, they reasoned, were hungry and laborious; was it not right and just that a better world should exist somewhere else? A thing that was difficult to determine was the attitude of the pigs towards

Moses. They all declared contemptuously that his stories about Sugarcandy Mountain were lies, and yet they allowed him to remain on the farm, not working, with an allowance of a gill of beer a day.

After his hoof had healed up, Boxer worked harder than ever. Indeed, all the animals worked like slaves that year. Apart from the regular work of the farm, and the rebuilding of the windmill, there was the schoolhouse for the young pigs, which was started in March. Sometimes the long hours on insufficient food were hard to bear, but Boxer never faltered. In nothing that he said or did was there any sign that his strength was not what it had been. It was only his appearance that was a little altered; his hide was less shiny than it had used to be, and his great haunches seemed to have shrunken. The others said, 'Boxer will pick up when the spring grass comes on'; but the spring came and Boxer grew no fatter. Sometimes on the slope leading to the top of the quarry, when he braced his muscles against the weight of some vast boulder, it seemed that nothing kept him on his feet except the will to continue. At such times his lips were seen to form the words, 'I will work harder'; he had no voice left. Once again Clover and Benjamin warned him to take care of his health, but Boxer paid no attention. His twelfth birthday was approaching. He did not care what happened so long as a good store of stone was accumulated before he went on pension.

Late one evening in the summer, a sudden rumour ran round the farm that something had happened to Boxer. He had gone out alone to drag a load of stone down to the windmill. And sure enough, the rumour was true. A few minutes later two pigeons came racing in with the news: 'Boxer has fallen! He is lying on his side and can't get up!'

About half the animals on the farm rushed out to the knoll where the windmill stood. There lay Boxer, between the shafts of the cart, his neck stretched out, unable even to raise his head. His eyes were glazed, his sides matted with sweat. A thin stream of blood had trickled out of his mouth. Clover dropped to her knees at his side.

'Boxer!' she cried, 'how are you?'

'It is my lung,' said Boxer in a weak voice. 'It does not matter. I think you will be able to finish the windmill without me. There is a pretty good store of stone accumulated. I had only another month to go in any case. To tell you the truth, I had been looking forward to my retirement. And perhaps, as Benjamin is growing old too, they will let him retire at the same time and be a companion to me.'

'We must get help at once,' said Clover. 'Run, somebody, and tell Squealer what has happened.'

All the other animals immediately raced back to the farm-house to give Squealer the news. Only Clover remained, and Benjamin, who lay down at Boxer's side, and, without speaking, kept the flies off him with his long tail. After about a quarter of an hour Squealer appeared, full of sympathy and concern. He said that Comrade Napoleon had learned with the very deepest distress of this misfortune to one of the most loyal workers on the farm, and was already making arrangements to send Boxer to be treated in the hospital at Willingdon. The animals felt a little uneasy at this. Except for Mollie and Snowball, no other animal had ever left the farm, and they did not like to think of their sick comrade in the hands of human beings. However, Squealer easily convinced them that the veterinary surgeon in Willingdon could treat Boxer's case more satisfactorily than could be done on the farm. And about half an hour later, when Boxer had somewhat recovered, he was with difficulty got on to his feet, and managed to limp back to his stall, where Clover and Benjamin had prepared a good bed of straw for him.

For the next two days Boxer remained in his stall. The pigs had sent out a large bottle of pink medicine which they had found in the medicine chest in the bathroom, and Clover administered it to Boxer twice a day after meals. In the evenings she lay in his stall and talked to him, while Benjamin kept the flies off him. Boxer professed not to be sorry for what had happened. If he made a good recovery, he might expect to live another three years, and he looked forward to the peaceful days that he would spend in the corner of the big pasture. It would be the first time that he had had leisure to study and improve his mind. He intended, he said, to devote the rest of his life to learning the remaining twenty-two letters of the alphabet.

However, Benjamin and Clover could only be with Boxer after working hours, and it was in the middle of the day when the van came to take him away. The animals were all at work weeding turnips under the supervision of a pig, when they were astonished to see Benjamin come galloping from the direction of the farm buildings, braying at the top of his voice. It was the first time that they had ever seen Benjamin excited—indeed, it was the first time that anyone had ever seen him gallop. 'Quick, quick!' he shouted. 'Come at once! They're taking Boxer away!' Without waiting for orders from the pig, the animals broke off work and raced back to the farm buildings. Sure enough, there in the yard was a large closed van, drawn by two horses, with lettering on its side and a sly-looking man in a low-crowned bowler hat sitting on the driver's seat. And Boxer's stall was empty.

The animals crowded round the van. 'Good-bye, Boxer!' they chorused, 'good-bye!'

'Fools! Fools!' shouted Benjamin, prancing round them and stamping the earth with his small hoofs. 'Fools! Do you not see what is written on the side of that van?'

That gave the animals pause, and there was a hush. Muriel began to spell out the words. But Benjamin pushed her aside and in the midst of a deadly silence he read:

' "Alfred Simmonds, Horse Slaughterer and Glue-Boiler, Willingdon. Dealer in Hides and Bone-Meal. Kennels

Supplied." Do you not understand what that means? They are taking Boxer to the knacker's!'

A cry of horror burst from all the animals. At this moment the man on the box whipped up his horses and the van moved out of the yard at a smart trot. All the animals followed, crying out at the tops of their voices. Clover forced her way to the front. The van began to gather speed. Clover tried to stir her stout limbs to a gallop, and achieved a canter. 'Boxer!' she cried. 'Boxer! Boxer! Boxer!' And just at this moment, as though he had heard the uproar outside, Boxer's face, with the white stripe down his nose, appeared at the small window at the back of the van.

'Boxer!' cried Clover in a terrible voice. 'Boxer! Get out! Get out quickly! They are taking you to your death!'

All the animals took up the cry of 'Get out, Boxer, get out!' But the van was already gathering speed and drawing away from them. It was uncertain whether Boxer had understood what Clover had said. But a moment later his face disappeared from the window and there was the sound of a tremendous drumming of hoofs inside the van. He was trying to kick his way out. The time had been when a few kicks from Boxer's hoofs would have smashed the van to matchwood. But alas! his strength had left him; and in a few moments the sound of drumming hoofs grew fainter and died away. In desperation the animals began appealing to the two horses which drew the van to stop. 'Comrades, comrades!' they shouted. 'Don't take your own brother to his death!' But the stupid brutes, too ignorant to realize what was happening, merely set back their ears and quickened their pace. Boxer's face did not reappear at the window. Too late, someone thought of racing ahead and shutting the five-barred gate; but in another moment the van was through it and rapidly disappearing down the road. Boxer was never seen again.

Three days later it was announced that he had died in the hospital at Willingdon, in spite of receiving every attention a horse could have. Squealer came to announce the news to the others. He had, he said, been present during Boxer's last hours.

'It was the most affecting sight I have ever seen!' said Squealer, lifting his trotter and wiping away a tear. 'I was at his bedside at the very last. And at the end, almost too weak to speak, he whispered in my ear that his sole sorrow was to have passed on before the windmill was finished. "Forward, comrades!" he whispered. 'Forward in the name of the Rebellion. Long live Animal Farm! Long live Comrade Napoleon! Napoleon is always right." Those were his very last words, comrades.'

Here Squealer's demeanour suddenly changed. He fell silent for a moment, and his little eyes darted suspicious glances from side to side before he proceeded.

It had come to his knowledge, he said, that a foolish and wicked rumour had been circulated at the time of Boxer's removal. Some of the animals had noticed that the van which took Boxer away was marked 'Horse Slaughterer', and had actually jumped to the conclusion that Boxer was being sent to the knacker's. It was almost unbelievable, said Squealer, that any animal could be so stupid. Surely, he cried indignantly, whisking his tail and skipping from side to side, surely they knew their beloved Leader, Comrade Napoleon, better than that? But the explanation was really very simple. The van had previously been the property of the knacker, and had been bought by the veterinary surgeon, who had not yet painted the old name out. That was how the mistake had arisen.

The animals were enormously relieved to hear this. And when Squealer went on to give further graphic details of Boxer's death bed, the admirable care he had received, and the expensive medicines for which Napoleon had paid without a thought as to the cost, their last doubts disappeared and the sorrow that they felt for their comrade's death was tempered by the thought that at least he had died happy.

Napoleon himself appeared at the meeting on the following

Sunday morning and pronounced a short oration in Boxer's honour. It had not been possible, he said, to bring back their lamented comrade's remains for interment on the farm, but he had ordered a large wreath to be made from the laurels in the farmhouse garden and sent down to be placed on Boxer's grave. And in a few days' time the pigs intended to hold a memorial banquet in Boxer's honour. Napoleon ended his speech with a reminder of Boxer's two favourite maxims, 'I will work harder' and 'Comrade Napoleon is always right'— maxims, he said, which every animal would do well to adopt as his own.

On the day appointed for the banquet, a grocer's van drove up from Willingdon and delivered a large wooden crate at the farmhouse. That night there was the sound of uproarious singing, which was followed by what sounded like a violent quarrel and ended at about eleven o'clock with a tremendous crash of glass. No one stirred in the farmhouse before noon on the following day, and the word went round that from somewhere or other the pigs had acquired the money to buy themselves another case of whisky.

CHAPTER 10

YEARS passed. The seasons came and went, the short animal lives fled by. A time came when there was no one who remembered the old days before the Rebellion, except Clover, Benjamin, Moses the raven, and a number of the pigs.

Muriel was dead; Bluebell, Jessie, and Pitcher were dead. Jones too was dead—he had died in an inebriates' home in another part of the country. Snowball was forgotten. Boxer was forgotten, except by the few who had known him. Clover was an old stout mare now, stiff in the joints, and with a tendency to rheumy eyes. She was two years past retiring age, but in fact no animal had ever actually retired. The talk of setting aside a corner of the pasture for superannuated animals had long since been dropped. Napoleon was now a mature boar of twenty-four stone. Squealer was so fat that he could with difficulty see out of his eyes. Only old Benjamin was much the same as ever, except for being a little greyer about the muzzle, and, since Boxer's death, more morose and taciturn than ever.

There were many more creatures on the farm now, though the increase was not so great as had been expected in earlier years. Many animals had been born to whom the Rebellion was only a dim tradition, passed on by word of mouth, and others had been bought who had never heard mention of such a thing before their arrival. The farm possessed three horses now besides Clover. They were fine upstanding beasts, willing workers and good comrades, but very stupid. None of them proved able to learn the alphabet beyond the letter B. They accepted everything that they were told about the Rebellion and the principles of Animalism, especially from Clover, for whom they had an almost filial respect; but it was doubtful whether they understood very much of it.

The farm was more prosperous now, and better organized: it had even been enlarged by two fields which had been bought from Mr. Pilkington. The windmill had been successfully completed at last, and the farm possessed a threshing machine and a hay elevator of its own, and various new buildings had been added to it. Whymper had bought himself a dogcart. The windmill, however, had not after all been used for generating electrical power. It was used for milling corn, and brought in a handsome money profit. The animals were hard at work building yet another windmill; when that one was finished, so it was said, the dynamos would be installed. But the luxuries of which Snowball had once taught the animals to dream, the stalls with electric light and hot and cold water, and the three-day week, were no longer talked about. Napoleon had denounced such ideas as contrary to the spirit of Animalism. The truest happiness, he said, lay in working hard and living frugally.

Somehow it seemed as though the farm had grown richer without making the animals themselves any richer—except, of course, for the pigs and the dogs. Perhaps this was partly because there were so many pigs and so many dogs. It was not that these creatures did not work, after their fashion. There was, as Squealer was never tired of explaining, endless work in the supervision and organization of the farm. Much of this work was of a kind that the other animals were too ignorant to understand. For example, Squealer told them that the pigs had to expend enormous labours every day upon mysterious things called 'files', 'reports', 'minutes', and 'memoranda'. These were large sheets of paper which had to be closely covered with writing, and as soon as they were so covered, they were burnt in the furnace. This was of the highest importance for the welfare of the farm, Squealer said. But still, neither pigs nor dogs produced any food by their own labour; and there were very many of them, and their appetites were always good.

As for the others, their life, so far as they knew, was as it had always been. They were generally hungry, they slept on straw, they drank from the pool, they laboured in the fields; in winter they were troubled by the cold, and in the summer by the flies. Sometimes the older ones among them racked their dim memories and tried to determine whether in the early days of the Rebellion, when Jones's expulsion was still recent, things had been better or worse than now. They could not remember. There was nothing with which they could compare their present lives: they had nothing to go upon except Squealer's lists of figures, which invariably demonstrated that everything was getting better and better. The animals found the problem insoluble; in any case, they had little time for speculating on such things now. Only old Benjamin professed to remember every detail of his long life and to know that things never had been, nor ever could be much better or much worse—hunger, hardship, and disappointment being, so he said, the unalterable law of life.

And yet the animals never gave up hope. More, they never lost, even for an instant, their sense of honour and privilege in being members of Animal Farm. They were still the only farm in the whole country—in all England!—owned and operated by animals. Not one of them, not even the youngest, not even the newcomers who had been brought from farms ten or twenty miles away, ever ceased to marvel at that. And when they heard the gun booming and saw the green flag fluttering at the masthead, their hearts swelled with imperishable pride, and the talk always turned towards the old heroic days, the expulsion of Jones, the writing of the Seven Commandments, the great battles in which the human invaders had been defeated. None of the old dreams had been abandoned. The Republic of the Animals which Major had foretold, when the green fields of England should be untrodden by human feet, was still believed in. Some day it was coming: it might not be soon, it might not be within the lifetime of any animal now living, but still it was coming. Even the tune of 'Beasts of England' was perhaps hummed secretly here and there: at any rate, it was a fact that every animal on the farm knew it, though no one would have dared to sing it aloud. It might be that their lives were hard and that not all of their hopes had been fulfilled; but they were conscious that they were not as other animals. If they were hungry, it was not from feeding tyrannical human beings; if they worked hard, at least they worked for themselves. No creature among them went upon two legs. No creature called any other creature 'Master'. All animals were equal.

One day in early summer Squealer ordered the sheep to follow him, and led them out to a piece of waste ground at the other end of the farm, which had become overgrown with birch saplings. The sheep spent the whole day there browsing at the leaves under Squealer's supervision. In the evening he returned to the farmhouse himself, but, as it was warm weather, told the sheep to stay where they were. It ended by their remaining there for a whole week, during which time the other animals saw nothing of them. Squealer was with them for the greater part of every day. He was, he said, teaching them to sing a new song, for which privacy was needed.

It was just after the sheep had returned, on a pleasant evening when the animals had finished work and were making their way back to the farm buildings, that the terrified neighing of a horse sounded from the yard. Startled, the animals stopped in their tracks. It was Clover's voice. She neighed again, and all the animals broke into a gallop and rushed into the yard. Then they saw what Clover had seen.

It was a pig walking on his hind legs.

Yes, it was Squealer. A little awkwardly, as though not quite used to supporting his considerable bulk in that position, but with perfect balance, he was strolling across the yard. And a moment later, out from the door of the farmhouse came a long file of pigs, all walking on their hind legs. Some did it better than others, one or two were even a trifle unsteady and looked as though they would have liked the support of a stick, but every one of them made his way right round the yard successfully. And finally there was a tremendous baying of dogs and a shrill crowing from the black cockerel, and out came Napoleon himself, majestically upright, casting haughty glances from side to side, and with his dogs gambolling round him.

He carried a whip in his trotter.

There was a deadly silence. Amazed, terrified, huddling together, the animals watched the long line of pigs march slowly round the yard. It was as though the world had turned

82

upside-down. Then there came a moment when the first shock had worn off and when, in spite of everything—in spite of their terror of the dogs, and of the habit, developed through long years, of never complaining, never criticizing, no matter what happened—they might have uttered some word of protest. But just at that moment, as though at a signal, all the sheep burst out into a tremendous bleating of—

'Four legs good, two legs *better*! Four legs good, two legs *better*! Four legs good, two legs *better*!'

It went on for five minutes without stopping. And by the time the sheep had quieted down, the chance to utter any protest had passed, for the pigs had marched back into the farmhouse.

Benjamin felt a nose nuzzling at his shoulder. He looked round. It was Clover. Her old eyes looked dimmer than ever. Without saying anything, she tugged gently at his mane and led him round to the end of the big barn, where the Seven Commandments were written. For a minute or two they stood gazing at the tarred wall with its white lettering.

'My sight is failing,' she said finally. 'Even when I was young I could not have read what was written there. But it appears to me that that wall looks different. Are the Seven Commandments the same as they used to be, Benjamin?'

For once Benjamin consented to break his rule, and he read out to her what was written on the wall. There was nothing there now except a single Commandment. It ran:

ALL ANIMALS ARE EQUAL
BUT SOME ANIMALS ARE MORE
EQUAL THAN OTHERS

After that it did not seem strange when next day the pigs who were supervising the work of the farm all carried whips in their trotters. It did not seem strange to learn that the pigs had bought themselves a wireless set, were arranging to install a telephone, and had taken out subscriptions to *John Bull, Tit-*

Bits, and the *Daily Mirror*. It did not seem strange when Napoleon was seen strolling in the farmhouse garden with a pipe in his mouth—no, not even when the pigs took Mr. Jones's clothes out of the wardrobes and put them on, Napoleon himself appearing in a black coat, rat-catcher breeches, and leather leggings, while his favourite sow appeared in the watered silk dress which Mrs. Jones had been used to wear on Sundays.

A week later, in the afternoon, a number of dog-carts drove up to the farm. A deputation of neighbouring farmers, had been invited to make a tour of inspection. They were shown all over the farm, and expressed great admiration for everything they saw, especially the windmill. The animals were weeding the turnip field. They worked diligently, hardly raising their faces from the ground, and not knowing whether to be more frightened of the pigs or of the human visitors.

That evening loud laughter and bursts of singing came from the farmhouse. And suddenly, at the sound of the mingled voices, the animals were stricken with curiosity. What could be happening in there, now that for the first time animals and human beings were meeting on terms of equality? With one accord they began to creep as quietly as possible into the farmhouse garden.

At the gate they passed, half frightened to go on, but Clover led the way in. They tiptoed up to the house, and such animals as were tall enough peered in at the dining-room window. There, round the long table, sat half a dozen farmers and half a dozen of the more eminent pigs, Napoleon himself occupying the seat of honour at the head of the table. The pigs appeared completely at ease in their chairs. The company had been enjoying a game of cards, but had broken off for a moment, evidently in order to drink a toast. A large jug was circulating, and the mugs were being refilled with beer. No one noticed the wondering faces of the animals that gazed in at the window.

Mr. Pilkington of Foxwood, had stood up, his mug in his hand. In a moment, he said, he would ask the present company to drink a toast. But before doing so, there were a few words that he felt it incumbent upon him to say.

It was a source of great satisfaction to him, he said—and, he was sure, to all others present—to feel that a long period of mistrust and misunderstanding had now come to an end. There had been a time—not that he, or any of the present company, had shared such sentiments—but there had been a time when the respected proprietors of Animal Farm had been regarded, he would not say with hostility, but perhaps with a certain measure of misgiving, by their human neighbours. Unfortunate incidents had occurred, mistaken ideas had been current. It had been felt that the existence of a farm owned and operated by pigs was somehow abnormal and was liable to have an unsettling effect in the neighbourhood. Too many farmers had assumed, without due inquiry, that on such a farm a spirit of licence and indiscipline would prevail. They had been nervous about the effects upon their own animals, or even upon their human employees. But all such doubts were now dispelled. Today he and his friends had visited Animal Farm and inspected every inch of it with their own eyes, and what did they find? Not only the most up-to-date methods, but a discipline and an orderliness which should be an example to all farmers everywhere. He believed that he was right in saying that the lower animals on Animal Farm did more work and received less food than any animals in the country. Indeed, he and his fellow-visitors today had observed many features which they intended to introduce on their own farms immediately.

He would end his remarks, he said, by emphasizing once again the friendly feelings that subsisted, and ought to subsist, between Animal Farm and its neighbours. Between pigs and human beings there was not, and there need not be, any clash of interests whatever. Their struggles and their difficulties were one. Was not the labour problem the same everywhere? Here it became apparent that Mr. Pilkington was about to spring some carefully prepared witticism on the company, but for a moment he was too overcome by amusement to be able to utter it. After much choking, during which his various chins turned purple, he managed to get it out: 'If you have your lower animals to contend with,' he said, 'we have our lower classes!' This *bon mot* set the table in a roar; and Mr. Pilkington once again congratulated the pigs on the low rations, the long working hours, and the general absence of pampering which he had observed on Animal Farm.

And now, he said finally, he would ask the company to rise on their feet and make certain that their glasses were full. 'Gentlemen,' concluded Mr. Pilkington, 'gentlemen, I give you a toast: to the prosperity of Animal Farm!'

There was enthusiastic cheering and stamping of feet. Napoleon was so gratified that he left his place and came round the table to clink his mug against Mr. Pilkington's before emptying it. When the cheering had died down, Napoleon, who had remained on his feet, intimated that he too had a few words to say.

Like all Napoleon's speeches, it was short and to the point. He too, he said, was happy that the period of misunderstanding was at an end. For a long time there had been rumours—circulated, he had reason to think, by some malignant enemy —that there was something subversive and even revolutionary in the outlook of himself and his colleagues. They had been credited with attempting to stir up rebellion among the animals on neighbouring farms. Nothing could be further from the truth! Their sole wish, now and in the past, was to live at peace and in normal business relations with their neighbours. This farm which he had the honour to control, he added, was a co-operative enterprise. The title-deeds, which were in his own possession, were owned by the pigs jointly.

He did not believe, he said, that any of the old suspicions still lingered, but certain changes had been made recently in the routine of the farm which should have the effect of promoting confidence still further. Hitherto the animals on the farm had had a rather foolish custom of addressing one another as 'Comrade'. This was to be suppressed. There had also been a very strange custom, whose origin was unknown, of marching every Sunday morning past a boar's skull which was nailed to a post in the garden. This, too, would be suppressed, and the skull had already been buried. His visitors might have observed, too, the green flag which flew from the masthead. If so, they would perhaps have noted that the white hoof and horn with which it had previously been marked had now been removed. It would be a plain green flag from now onwards.

He had only one criticism, he said, to make of Mr. Pilkington's excellent and neighbourly speech. Mr. Pilkington had referred throughout to 'Animal Farm'. He could not of course know—for he, Napoleon, was only now for the first time announcing it—that the name 'Animal Farm' had been abolished. Henceforward the farm was to be known as the 'Manor Farm'—which, he believed, was its correct and original name.

'Gentlemen,' concluded Napoleon, 'I will give you the same toast as before, but in a different form. Fill your glasses to the brim. Gentlemen, here is my toast: To the prosperity of the Manor Farm!'

There was the same hearty cheering as before, and the mugs were emptied to the dregs. But as the animals outside gazed at the scene, it seemed to them that some strange thing was happening. What was it that had altered in the faces of the pigs? Clover's old dim eyes flitted from one face to another. Some of them had five chins, some had four, some had three. But what was it that seemed to be melting and changing? Then, the applause having come to an end, the company took

87

up their cards and continued the game that had been interrupted, and the animals crept silently away.

But they had not gone twenty yards when they stopped short. An uproar of voices was coming from the farmhouse. They rushed back and looked through the window again. Yes, a violent quarrel was in progress. There were shoutings, bangings on the table, sharp suspicious glances, furious denials. The source of the trouble appeared to be that Napoleon and Mr. Pilkington had each played an ace of spades simultaneously.

Twelve voices were shouting in anger, and they were all alike. No question, now, what had happened to the faces of the pigs. The creatures outside looked from pig to man, and from man to pig, and from pig to man again; but already it was impossible to say which was which.

Notes

The notes in this edition are intended to serve the needs of overseas students as well as those of British-born users.

Chapter 1

1 *pop-holes:* small openings in the walls of a hen-house just big enough for a bird to pass through.

scullery: back kitchen; room for washing up dishes.

Middle White boar: Major belongs to a breed of pigs that appears sulky and aggressive.

Willingdon Beauty: Major's pedigree name; the name recorded at his birth because he is a carefully-bred pig. He is called after the nearby town.

ensconced: established; comfortably seated.

tushes: tusks.

2 *never quite got her figure back:* Clover is like a woman who having given birth to a child is unable to regain her slim, youthful body.

hands: units for measuring the height of horses. Each is four inches (about 10.2 cm).

cynical: sneering; without illusions about life or human behaviour.

paddock: small, fenced field for horses to graze and rest.

trap: small, two-wheeled open carriage.

mincing: walking in an affected, swaying manner.

flirting: displaying so as to attract attention.

3 *Comrades . . . :* Major speaks to the animals in the manner of a socialist or communist leader addressing a crowd. His speech is a simple statement of Marxist political theory *(see Introduction,* page xxi): the animals (or workers) labour but do not benefit from their work. All the benefits go to

Man (or the employers, the ruling-classes) who *consumes without producing*, that is, enjoys the products of labour without having worked for them.

4 *confinement:* time when a mother is giving birth to a baby.

natural span: period of time for which an animal might expect to live under normal conditions.

porkers: pigs bred for their meat.

scream your lives out at the block: pigs used to be killed by having their throats slit after which they would scream and bleed to death.

5 *knacker:* man who slaughters old horses and sells their meat.

All men are enemies. All animals are comrades: Major's political message is simple and stirring, just right for inspiring rebellion. Orwell delightfully reveals how hopelessly inadequate he sees it to be in the farcical episode that interrupts the speech (see *Introduction*, page xxvi).

6 *dissentients:* people who disagree with the view of the majority.

I cannot describe that dream: Major is an excellent orator. He adds a touch of mystery to his message and then whips up the feelings of his listeners by getting them to sing together. There is no time for a critical discussion of what he has said.

'Beasts of England': the song is a parody of the *Internationale*, the anthem of international communism: 'Arise, ye prisoners of starvation! Arise, ye slaves, no more in thrall . . .'

7 *'Clementine' and 'La Cucuracha':* the first is an old ballad-style song and the second is a modern South American dance-band tune, an uneasy mixture.

bit and spur: metal mouthpiece for restraining a horse and sharply pointed piece of metal, attached to a rider's heel, for urging a horse forward.

mangel-wurzels: large root vegetables, used as cattle food.

8 *lowed . . . whined . . . bleated . . . whinnied . . . quacked:* words which convey the sounds made by the different animals.

Chapter 2

9 *Major died peacefully:* Marx never lived to see the Russian Revolution. He died in 1883 and it was left to others to carry out the revolution he had inspired.

breeding up for sale: these pigs are being kept and fed until fully mature for breeding purposes and then Jones will sell them.

Snowball and Napoleon: Orwell contrasts their characters. Snowball is a clever theorist and an idealist concerned for the welfare of the other animals whilst Napoleon has, from the start, a lust for power and self-indulgence, like his great historical name-sake. Neither pig corresponds exactly with a particular communist leader though the rivalry between them parallels that which broke out between Trotsky and Stalin after Lenin's death in 1924.

black into white: Squealer is clever enough to make even evil seem good and is thus perfectly cast as Napoleon's public-relations man and propaganda chief.

a complete system of thought: this is the second stage of revolutionary activity, when the ideas of the leader are developed and spread amongst the people by his followers. There was much activity of this sort in Russia before the revolution.

10 *Mollie:* perhaps stands for the vain, self-indulgent parasites and servants of the Tsar's court. *Moses* is clearly the Church, the priesthood.

linseed cake: solid mass of seeds fed to birds in captivity. Moses' heaven is particularly pleasant for ravens.

the two cart-horses: large, muscular horses bred for farm work. Boxer and Clover are representatives of the simple peasants who crave a better way of life and loyally support those who appear to be concerned for them.

11 *he had fallen on evil days:* there had been considerable economic difficulty and bad government in Russia in the years leading up to 1917. The country had also been weakened

by its involvement in the First World War as Jones had been by his lawsuit.

Windsor chair: wooden armchair of a style frequently found in nineteenth-century English farmhouses.

Midsummer's Eve: June 23rd, and traditionally a night for wild revels.

rabbiting: shooting wild rabbits.

News of the World: a famous popular English Sunday newspaper.

12 *carpet-bag:* a travelling bag made out of hard-wearing cloth, like carpet.

harness-room: this corresponds to the prisons and palaces of the aristocracy. The people attacked and entered the Winter Palace in St Petersburg in 1917 and there was a similar famous occasion in the storming of the Bastille in 1789 at the start of the French Revolution.

castrate: animals being bred for their meat are operated on so as to prevent their producing any off-spring.

threw on to the fire the ribbons: a parallel may be found in the abandonment of the Tsar's system of honours and decorations which were worn on public occasions.

13 *knoll:* little hill.

spinney: small wood.

14 *horsehair sofa:* long seat with arms and stuffed with horse-hair for more than one person to sit on.

Brussels carpet: the Belgians were famous makers of carpets.

lithographs: A lithograph is a kind of picture made by taking a print from a prepared flat block of polished stone on which a drawing has been treated with water and ink.

drawing-room: in a farmhouse, this would be the best sitting-room.

mantelpiece: the stone or wood surround and shelf over a fireplace.

Some hams . . . were taken out for burial: since they were, of course, the remains of dead comrades.

15 *reducing the principles of Animalism to Seven Commandments.*
Orwell's criticism of propaganda is clear. The title of the
system is itself designed to arouse national feeling and a
false sense of exclusiveness. It is based on fear of man as
the ever-present enemy and it is to this that Squealer will
always refer in the future to overcome any animal opposition. The system is false too because it pays no attention
to individual needs and its principles are not carefully
thought out. It is important to give due attention to the
Commandments since the development of the novel turns
on the successive perversion of both the spirit and the letter of each one.

Chapter 3

16 *mowing and raking:* cutting grass and gathering it up into
heaps.

17 *Gee up . . . Whoa back:* phrases used when shouting to a
horse; the first meaning to move faster and the second to
slow down or come to a standstill.
worthless parasitical human beings: the phrase reflects Marx's
view of the capitalists, the owners, as being parasites who
live off the efforts of the workers. In these early idealistic
days, the revolutionaries' language still means something.
cockerels: young cocks.

18 *bushels:* measures of capacity. A bushel is 8 gallons or 36.3
litres.
Donkeys live a long time: Benjamin has had more experience
and can see further than the other animals and he knows
that the revolution will not ultimately improve their lot.
He believes that all a man can do is to preserve his own
skin.
cryptic answer: mysterious brief utterance.
a hoof and a horn: a witty parallel to the flag of the Soviet
Union with its hammer and sickle, signs which symbolise

the union of the industrial workers with the rural peasantry.

the future Republic of the Animals: just as Snowball was not content with overthrowing humans on Manor Farm but wished to extend the revolution, so Marx himself had proposed a world-wide communist revolution, an ideal also fostered by Trotsky.

the meeting: in Russia in the early days of the revolution, such meetings were an important and valuable feature of life on the big collective farms.

19 *Animal Committees:* many 'Workers' Committees' were established by Trotsky immediately after the Soviet Revolution. Their purpose was to educate the illiterate masses and spread the principles of Marxism.

20 *faculty:* ability or skill at something.

maxim: slogan or motto.

21 *an organ of propulsion and not of manipulation:* means of moving forward and not a means of handling something. Orwell delightfully mocks the abstract language used by politicians to justify their beliefs.

Chapter 4

23 *flights of pigeons:* the work of pigeons in spreading news of the revolution is parallel to that of communist infiltrators and sympathisers working in non-communist countries.

Foxwood . . . Pinchfield: the two neighbouring farms suggest the countries of Britain and Germany respectively. World reaction to the Russian Revolution passed through the various stages of alarm, scorn, exaggeration and real fear which are outlined by Orwell in these paragraphs.

24 *cannibalism:* the eating of its own kind by humans or animals.

in common: available for the whole community to use; not limited to an individual. There is a reference here to the arrangements for easy divorce available in the Soviet Union for a short time after the revolution.

tractable: gentle and easy to control.

hunters refused their fences: horses trained for racing or fox-hunting refused to jump over fences or other obstacles that their riders wished them to clear.

smithies: workshops where metal objects such as horse-shoes and farming tools are made.

25 *an old book of Julius Caesar's campaigns:* probably Caesar's *Commentaries* in translation, describing, among others, his conquests of Gaul and Britain.

muted: discharged their droppings.

a light skirmishing manoeuvre: a brief, carefully-planned, small-scale battle.

hobnailed boots: boots with heavy-headed nails in their soles.

26 *his fifteen stone:* his full weight (95.25 kg).

27 *horse-brasses:* ornamental brass discs used to decorate the harness of a horse.

posthumously: after death.

28 *October the twelfth:* the seizing of power in Russia by the Bolsheviks is known as 'the October Revolution'. It was on the night of 12−13 October 1918 that a cavalry corps supporting the government was defeated outside Moscow, thus securing the position of the new leaders who had seized power four days earlier.

Chapter 5

28 *pretext:* excuse.

29 *dogcart:* small, two-wheeled driving-cart.

check breeches: short trousers fastened below the knee made from material with a pattern of coloured squares on it.

gaiters: leather coverings for the legs below the knee.

manifestly: obviously.

acreage: area of land (1 acre = 4046.9 square metres).

canvassing: obtaining votes and promises of support.

30 *Farmer and Stockbreeder:* a weekly journal for farmers.

field-drains: pipes buried in a field so as to allow excess water to be drained and the land improved.

silage: fermented vegetable matter put into deep pits to be used as winter feeding for animals.

basic slag: an industrial waste product which is used as fertiliser by farmers.

the windmill: the planning and building of the windmill corresponds to the first of the Soviet Union's Five Year Plans (1928) in which heavy industries received preference over the production of consumer goods.

incubators: apparatus for hatching birds and rearing them in artificial heat.

31 *closeted:* shut away to discuss or study privately.

cranks and cog-wheels: pieces of machinery; shafts and wheels for transmitting power or motion.

factions: militant political parties.

32 *Snowball and Napoleon were in disagreement:* the two main issues are the economy and foreign policy. Snowball wants industrial development whilst Napoleon appears at this stage to be advocating the growth of agriculture rather than heavy industry. Snowball still holds by the Marxist ideal of world-wide revolution whilst Napoleon wants to concentrate on developing national strength. The Soviet Union did, under Stalin, pursue the latter policy. Snowball eloquently offers the animals a paradise where all drudgery would be carried out by machines but Napoleon wins by the weapons of a dictator: the sheep bleat for him, like the disciplined cheers at a Nazi rally, and the dogs, his secret police or storm-troopers, frighten the other animals.

33 *Snowball . . . was seen no more:* the expulsion of Snowball may be compared with the exile of Trotsky from the Soviet Union in 1927.

34 *a special committee of pigs:* so the revolution enters a new phase with absolute control being assumed by a group of senior party officials who increasingly enjoy additional privileges and material comfort.

Squealer was sent round the farm: just as Napoleon becomes the party chief and withdraws and becomes aloof, so Squealer becomes the propaganda chief, his job being to explain away all the changes of policy.

35 *Napoleon is always right:* the remote political leader becomes idolised by the suffering but ignorant peasants who follow him blindly.

The skull of old Major: although, generally speaking, Major's role corresponds with that of Karl Marx, this incident recalls the placing on permanent display in a mausoleum in Moscow of Lenin's mummified body after his death in 1924.

36 *manoeuvre:* trick

Chapter 6

38 *governess-cart:* light two-wheeled cart with side seats face to face, where the children could sit and be easily watched by their governess.

39 *arable land:* land on which crops are grown rather than *pasture*, which is grass-land for animals to graze on.

40 *solicitor:* a kind of lawyer who advises clients.

41 *broker:* middleman or agent in business.

never . . . with both simultaneously: Stalin similarly toyed with different alliances at the same time. In March 1939, he was still denouncing Hitler, yet in August of the same year, he signed a peace pact with Germany while he was actually negotiating a mutual alliance with Britain and France.

42 *sleep in a bed with sheets:* gradually the pigs change all the commandments and lose the original ideals of the revolu-

tion as the dictator increasingly seeks his own personal comfort.

44 *Snowball!:* Napoleon is able to make Snowball appear to be the cause of all the evils they suffer by mounting a smear campaign against him. Only the all-powerful leader is in a position to save his people from this imaginary enemy: it is a characteristic pose of the dictator.

Chapter 7

46 *clamps:* piles of vegetables covered by straw and earth so as to preserve them.

infanticide: murder of new-born babies.

47 *clutches:* sets of eggs for hatching.

Black Minorca pullets: young fowls of a breed which origin-ally came from Minorca, the island in the Mediterranean.

their eggs ... smashed to pieces: the destructive revolt of the hens corresponds to the opposition of the kulaks, land-owning peasants, to Stalin's formation of farming collec-tives. In 1929 they burnt their farms and killed their cattle rather than that they should fall into the hands of the gov-ernment.

coccidiosis: a serious disease of poultry.

49 *He snuffed in every corner:* Stalin, too, rigorously pursued and eliminated potential opposition to his power in the 1930s.

blood-curdling: terrifying; sufficiently frightening to congeal the blood (metaphorically).

50 *formulate:* put into words; clearly express.

51 *categorically:* with absolute clarity and certainty.

52 *they confessed ... in touch with Snowball:* in August 1936 Stalin charged a group of Communist Party officials with being Trotskyists and with plotting with enemy powers outside Russia. To the amazement of the rest of the world, they confessed to these charges and were executed. This was

the first of a great series of 'show trials' in the years between 1936 and 1938. It was later proved that the confessions were the result of brainwashing and torture.

confessions and executions went on: the brainwashing is so effective that not only are the dissidents punished but even the innocent are drawn into the blood-purge.

55 *this song has no longer any purpose:* with the establishment of the totalitarian communist state, the leader declares the revolution to be complete. No longer is there any serious attempt to achieve world-wide revolution: the anthem of international communism is replaced by a national anthem.

Chapter 8

56 *lists of figures:* statistics can be made to prove anything as the Soviet authorities demonstrated in the 1930s.

57 *Napoleon himself was not seen in public:* this assuming of a god-like remoteness, of elaborate ritualised appearances and a string of meaningless titles is typical of the totalitarian leader.

Crown Derby dinner service: valuable porcelain dishes, made at Derby in the north of England.

58 *swill-bucket:* a bucket in which is kept discarded food to be fed in watered mixture to pigs.

skulking: hiding a shameful way.

59 *the rumours of an impending treacherous attack:* these may be compared with the gathering fears of a Nazi invasion of Russia before the Second World War.

terrible stories: the rumours of the persecution of Jews and others in Nazi Germany were, of course, proved to be horrifically true.

cocks fight: cock fighting was banned in England. It consisted of setting cocks with sharp weapons attached to their legs to attack each other.

60 *privy to:* aware of the secret.

deadly nightshade: a wild plant with purple flowers and highly poisonous berries.

61 *he had sold the pile to Frederick:* see note to *never . . . with both simultaneously,* page 41. ·

pensioner: someone who receives money or support from a patron. After his exile from the Soviet Union, Trotsky lived in Mexico until his assassination there in 1940.

63 *the whole of the big pasture . . . hands of the enemy:* Hitler invaded the Soviet Union in June 1941 and advanced to the gates of Moscow. Great destruction and loss of life occurred, particularly at the battle for Stalingrad, and it was not until the spring of 1944 that Russian soil was cleared of German invaders.

65 *That is our victory:* Orwell emphasises the futility of war and victory celebrations. The animals suffer material destruction, wounding and deaths and only end up with the land they previously possessed anyway.

Chapter 9

68 *poultices:* soft masses made with boiling water and placed on wounded flesh to help it heal.

69 *superannuated:* sent into retirement with a pension.

a readjustment of rations: Orwell is merciless with language which is used to disguise reality for propaganda purposes.

70 *The young pigs:* and so a new, self-perpetuating and privileged ruling class, set apart from the rest of the people, is established.

71 *Spontaneous Demonstration:* the display of military might and a long march is the main feature of the May Day parades in Moscow which also involve 'a lot of waiting about in the cold'.

72 *Moses the raven suddenly reappeared:* as did the orthodox priests in Russia, where they are similarly tolerated, though officially condemned because they provide comfort for the people and so reduce discontent.

73 *haunches:* the part of the body between the thighs and bottom ribs, the back part of the horse's body.

75 *low-crowned bowler hat:* a hard felt black hat with a dome-like crown and curved brims.

77 *demeanour:* bearing; awkward behaviour.

Horse Slaughterer: note the sad irony of Boxer's end. It is exactly what old Major had forecast for him under the rule of Jones (see page 5).

78 *oration:* a formal speech or address.

Chapter 10

78 *an inebriates' home:* place where alcoholics, people who have a drink problem, are treated and looked after.

79 *rheumy eyes:* eyes that run with a watery fluid.

filial: the relationship of a child with its parents.

The windmill . . . was used for milling corn: so the ideal of isolation from the profit-making capitalist world is abandoned and the economy of the communist country becomes the same as that of its neighbours.

80 *'files', 'reports', 'minutes' and 'memoranda':* all the apparatus of bureaucracy and official paper work. *Minutes* are records of meetings and *memoranda* are the directives that officials send to one another. Orwell suggests that this work is worthless and unproductive, only existing to give the pigs an easy life.

83 *wireless set:* radio.

John Bull: a British weekly magazine aimed at a family readership.

84 *Daily Mirror:* a very popular London daily newspaper.

rat-catcher trousers: full-cut trousers which fit close to the leg from the knees downwards, worn by sportsmen and farmers.

watered silk: silk material which reflects light in a pattern like waves on water.

A deputation of neighbouring farmers: the meeting with the party of human visitors, led by Pilkington, who proposes the toast, suggests the Allied conference at Teheran in December 1943. (See *Introduction*, page xxv.)

85 *felt it incumbent upon him:* felt it to be his duty; felt obliged.

86 *bon mot:* witty remark.

title-deeds: documents proving the ownership of a property. Napoleon's boast of possession suggests that government in a communist country is, in the end, handled in much the same way as it is in capitalist countries.

Study questions

1 Write character studies of Napoleon, Snowball and Squealer bringing out how their actions in the novel reveal the types of personality that they are.

2 What are the turning points in the novel? Discuss the main events of the plot and show how the reader's sympathies are affected by each one.

3 How many conflicts can you find in *Animal Farm*? How does Orwell use these various conflicts to point his moral, that political ideals collapse and give way to tyranny?

4 How do the following animals help us to understand Orwell's criticism of the 'Soviet myth': Boxer, Clover, the sheep, Benjamin, Moses? Write about each in turn explaining their actions in the novel and how they affect the reader's feelings and political understanding.

5 *Animal Farm* is both an exposure of the 'Soviet myth' – a criticism of Stalin and his policies – and an exposure of the nature of revolution itself. Describe some incidents from the novel which can be related to Russian history and which also prompt you to question human nature and to think about broader issues.

6 In the introduction you will find a commentary on some amusing episodes from the novel (see pages xxv–xxviii). Find some other amusing moments in the novel and show how Orwell uses humour to bring home his points.